TERROR

WIGGOTT'S WONDERFUL WAXWORLD

TRAIN

TERRY DEARY

SCHOLASTIC

Scholastic Children's Books
An imprint of Scholastic Ltd
Euston House, 24 Eversholt Street, London, NW1 1DB, UK
Registered office: Westfield Road, Southam, Warwickshire, CV47 0RA
SCHOLASTIC and associated logos are trademarks and/or
registered trademarks of Scholastic Inc.

First published in the UK by Scholastic Ltd, 2018

ISBN 978 1407 17934 6

A CIP catalogue record for this book
is available from the British Library.

Printed by CPI Group (UK) Ltd, Croydon, CR0 4YY
Papers used by Scholastic Children's Books are made
from wood grown in sustainable forests.

1 3 5 7 9 10 8 6 4 2

www.scholastic.co.uk

This book is dedicated to all those amazing children and young people who have fought or are fighting cancer.

Terry is raising money for the CLIC Sargent fund for those children and one brave little boy in particular. Find out more and about how to donate at terry-deary.com

Contents

I think they lock people away in there

In the dark and seedy streets of the town there were twisted towers of flats and factories. They were the colour of smoke-brown and concrete. They were greasy, grey and dismal as a wet Sunday. But one building stood tall and shining, glittering glass. It was the sort of glass that you could see your face in[1] ... but you couldn't see inside. You couldn't see *through* the special glass.

The glittering, pointy tower had been built in a matter of weeks. The people of Wildpool waited to see what would happen. And the answer was ... very little. Very little to *see*.

---

1 If you ever forget what your face looks like.

Workers in white rode their bikes into the underground car park at nine o'clock every morning. They rode out again at five o'clock each evening. But they never said what they did inside each day.

'What do you DO in there?' the good folk of Wildpool cried.

'It's a secret,' the white-coated, blank-faced workers mumbled and pedalled off into the sunset. A sunset that turned the glass tower a glowing red ... like blood.

There was a café opposite Loaf Tower. Edna Crudge and her two ancient friends had breakfast with her every morning at eight. They called themselves 'The Ladies Who Crunch'. They nodded as they chewed their scones with clattering teeth.

'So what's in there, Edna?' little Minnie Cooper asked.

'It's a factory full of secrets,' Mrs Crudge said. 'Secret gadgets. I know. Mr Crudge works in the world of gadgets. His friends tell him when someone is making an incredible new invention.'

'And what is Arfur Loaf making?' her best

friend Marjorie Doors asked as her knitting needles clacked louder and faster than her teeth.

'I will say you when you need to know,' Edna Crudge told her. Edna had a face that said, 'Don't argue.' Marjorie had a face that said, 'You're a bossy fuss-pot, Edna.' (But she didn't say it out loud.)

Little Minnie Cooper twittered, 'Well I think it's a prison. I think they lock people away in there.' Whenever Minnie spoke she seemed to shiver.

Edna Crudge snorted. 'Prisons have bars.'

'Is that so the prisoners can get beer?' Marjorie Doors asked.

Edna looked down her thin nose and sneered. 'Not *beer* bars. Iron bars. Prisons have iron bars to keep the villains in. There's no bars in that there glass tower, so there's no prisoners. *Humph!*'

Edna Crudge was right about the inventions. But Edna Crudge was as wrong as wrong can be about the prisoners. And Minnie Copper was as right as right . . . in a way.

The glass tower was the place a boy had arrived at eight o'clock that very morning to make the steal of the century. . .

Can you let me through?

'**A** prison?' you cry. 'The boy who is planning the steal-of-the-century is walking into a prison? Why?' you cry[2].

The boy took one last look at the crumpled paper in his hand. It read...

> <u>BOY.</u>
>
> GO TO THE LOAF COMPANY TOWER.
> THE CHAIRMAN, ARFUR LOAF, IS GOING TO SHOW AN
> IMPORTANT VISITOR, LADY GREYSTONE, A NEW MOBILE
> PHONE KNOWN AS THE INFINIT-G.

---

2 You seem to do a lot of crying, don't you? I hope you have a lot of tissues handy.

STEAL THAT PHONE.

DELIVER THE PHONE TO DR WIGGOTT AT HIS WAXWORLD MUSEUM – USE THE BACK DOOR IN DANK ALLEY.

DR WIGGOTT WILL PAY YOU A THOUSAND POUNDS WHEN YOU HAND IT OVER.

HOW YOU DO THE THEFT IS UP TO YOU. YOU ARE THE BEST THIEF IN THE CRIME COLLEGE.

BUT DON'T GET CAUGHT. THE CHAIRMAN, ARFUR LOAF, IS A CRUEL MAN.

SIGNED: THE MASTER-THIEF

The thief, known only as 'Boy', tugged at the collar of his shirt and loosened his navy tie. He wasn't used to wearing a tie, but it was all part of the plan. Not just any old plan, but The Plan.

He looked at the small brass sign by the great glass doors. The sign read *The Loaf Company – Visitors report to security.*

Now you and I would sneak into the factory to steal a new phone, wouldn't we? We'd creep under barriers and pick locks and stun the guards with stun guns. We'd wear black clothes and masks over our faces.

Boy did none of these. He walked down the ramp into the underground bicycle park. He walked alongside the workers on their cycles. He walked in as bold as brass ... as bold as the brass on the Loaf Company sign. He wore a smart suit that matched his dark tie. He pushed a trolley with a shining tea urn and rattling cups. He carried a hooded top, rolled up, under his arm.

When he reached the underground entrance he joined the queue of white-coated workers. One by one they rubbed a plastic card against a panel and the gate clicked open.

Boy smiled at the guard. 'Morning,' he grinned. 'Can you let me through with the new tea trolley?'

'Where's your pass?'

'In my pocket. But I can't get it out while I'm pushing this trolley, can I? Let me in and I'll show you my pass later.'

The rock-faced guard sighed. He opened the gate. Boy walked in. Easy as pie. Just what you'd expect from the best thief in the crime college.

I'll get him, don't you worry. Heh! Heh! Heh!

When Arfur Loaf grew angry, his voice was not as big as his bear-like body. His hair was thick and black as a bear's too ... a black bear, obviously, not a polar, grizzly or koala bear. But his voice squeaked. He had just started a speech with the grand words, 'Lady Greystoke, let me show you the world's most amazing phone ... the infinit-G.' A jiggling-chinned woman in a scarlet dress stared with a look as hard as her red fingernails. When she moved, her jewellery crackled. When she frowned, her face crackled.

'It looks like any other mobile phone to me, Mr Loaf.'

'Wait and see, Lady Greystoke, wait and see,' the large man said.

At that moment, the tea-boy stepped between him and the phone. 'What are you doing, boy?' he squeak-squawked.

Loaf was standing next to a glass case. Inside the case lay a girl – as asleep as Sleeping Beauty. Boy saw a glimpse of reddish hair tied in pigtails. Wires sprouted from her head like quills from a porcupine. Arfur Loaf moved his large body to block the boy's view.

The boy-thief placed the teacup next to a phone that sat on a satin cushion on a table. He smiled brightly and said, 'Topper's Tea Trays at your service. Topper's top teas for top people and … may I say, sir … they don't come any more tip-top than you and your rich guest.' He nodded towards the lady in the scarlet dress who wore diamonds on her fingers and rubies round her wide neck.

Arfur Loaf puffed out his chest like a Baja California tree frog puffs out its throat.

'If I can just move this phone out of the way,' Boy said.

The phone felt itself being swept up in the boy's bone-thin, bone-hard, bone-white hand and thrust into a fluff-filled pocket. Loaf squeaked, 'Careful with that precious phone.'

Boy placed his teacups on the table next to the cushion. 'There you are, sir, safe as the crown jewels.'

But the phone knew it wasn't where it was supposed to be. Whatever was sitting on Loaf's cushion, it wasn't the infinit-G phone. The boy had done a switch. The phone knew he was a thief and she was being stolen[3]. Something in the phone's brain said, 'I've been stolen.' And something else in her micro-brain said, 'I'm not an *it*, I'm a *she*.'

The phone heard tea being poured. It heard lips sucking at the rims of cups. Heard spluttering and voices muttering, 'This tea's cold,' and 'This tea is just plain water.' Finally, the phone heard Arfur Loaf cry, 'Get out of here, tea-boy, we have important work.'

---

3 A top tip if you want to become a thief and steal the famous *Mona Lisa* painting: swap it for a fake. By the time the owners spot the difference, you're long gone. See? You'll learn more from this book than you would in ten years of school.

9

'Yes, sir,' the boy replied.

The phone felt itself jogged as Boy ran from the room and down the stairs, so she could tell she was moving. She heard the soft fluffle of another coat being thrown over the blue servant suit and guessed the thief was at the door when he shouted, 'Guard?'

'What you want, boy?'

'In a minute you'll get a call from Mr Loaf. He will say a boy has stolen a phone. He's a boy in a smart blue suit ... not an old hooded top like me.'

'A theft? A theft?' the guard growled. 'He'll never get past me.'

'He will,' Boy said, 'If you stay here. The lad will head for the front door.'

'I'll get him, don't you worry. Heh! Heh! Heh!' the guard laughed madly.

'Wait!' Boy cried. 'Let me out at this underground door first.'

'Go on, Sonny Jim, hurry up. I've got a thief to catch.' The door clicked open. Then the guard's feet beat a path away to the front door. The boy ... who was named in the note as 'Boy' ...

whistled softly.

The phone in the guard's room jangled loud. 'Too late,' Boy chuckled. 'The clever bird has flown ... flown to Wiggott's Wonderful Waxworld.'

It's better **you** get hurt than **me**

Arfur Loaf took three minutes to discover the switch. He raged till his face was as red as his guest's dress. 'Sorry, Lady Greystoke, there's a little problem.'

'Then solve it, Mr Loaf. Problems are there to be solved.' She had a chin under her chin and it jiggled when she was angry. It was jiggling now.

Loaf picked up a phone – not the stolen one ... which had been stolen. It took another five minutes to explain the problem to the police. It seemed that most of the Wildpool police force was out on a tricky task that morning.

'My beautiful phone, Igon,' Loaf hissed at his evil assistant.

The small man with a black eyepatch said, 'It was MY phone, Mr Loaf ... I invented it ... and my name is I-gor.'

'Your eye is gone ... so you will always be I-gon to me,' the cruel man sneered. 'You may have had the *idea* for the phone, but it was my money that let you make it. Whose money was it, Igon?'

'Yours, Mr Loaf, sir.'

'And what are the police and my security guards doing? How long will it be before I get my phone back?'

'Our guards have looked at the security cameras,' Igon explained, 'and it looks as if a boy stole it.' Mr Loaf's phone rang. Igon picked it up and listened. 'A message from the Wildpool police says they have a Constable Elloe on the thief's trail, sir. They think it's a boy from a local crime college. Elloe has tracked him down already.'

Arfur Loaf screamed till the desk shook. 'A constable? I want our top detectives, not a mere *constable*. I want the boy caught and hanged.'

'Erm … I don't think they do hanging any more, Mr Loaf,' the little eyepatched man muttered. 'And the police don't know what they are looking for,' he reminded the large man.

'Looking for? Looking for? The thief.' He lowered his voice. 'If they won't hang him, then I will find a very good use for him. A use for him in our lab. A place for him alongside the girl. Know what I mean?'

'Yes, sir. But the police don't know it's a *phone* he's stolen. You refused to tell them what is missing, remember?' Igon reminded his boss.

'Of course, of course I do … it's a secret. No one must know. We don't want the police snooping around here, DO we? You know what they'll find, DON'T you?'

'Yes, sir.'

'So where is this *Constable* Elloe?' Arfur Loaf spat.

'He's tracked the thief to a place called Wiggott's Wonderful Waxworld,' Igon said.

Arfur loaf turned pale, he turned red, he turned purple, he turned pale again[4]. 'Wiggott? Not *Wiggott*. Dr Wiggott is the cleverest inventor

---

4 His face would have been useful at a party as flashing disco lights, if you ask me.

in Wildpool. If Wiggott ever lays a hand on my infinit-G, we are finished, Igon, finished. It all makes sense. Wiggott ordered the robbery. Wiggott is a dangerous person,' Loaf breathed. 'Get down to the Waxworld at once and get my phone.'

'Why me?' Igon trembled.

'Because it's dangerous. Someone could get hurt. It's better *you* get hurt than *me*. It's on the High Street. Go now.'

'Yes, sir.' Igon dragged his feet towards the door. He went snail-slow, but he went. 'I'll call in the police station first,' he decided. 'No point in risking my life with this wild and wicked Wiggott.'

Arfur Loaf turned his large head with the hair of a bear towards Lady Greystone. 'A little glitch, a gremlin, a bug, a hiccup, a blip. I'll have it sorted in no time. Cup of tea?'

'It's cold water.'

'Ah. Yes. Sorry.'

I mean no **normal** people don't know

Arfur Loaf's great glass tower in the middle of Wildpool town stood like a fine flower in a mud patch. It just looked w-r-o-n-g. The dull town had twisted streets of grey-brown buildings and was as old as the muddy river that ran under the bow-legged bridges. The tower was new and sparkling in the sun that flitted through the fire-fogged air.

The Ladies Who Crunch sat outside the café with dust-stained windows and looked across at Loaf Tower. Edna Crudge gave a tiny smile when she saw Boy, in his hooded top, slip out of the building and hurry towards the shadowy side of town. Then she turned back to the smartphone on the table and looked at the news page. 'They haven't found that missing girl yet,' she muttered through her mean mouth. Edna had arms like a boxer[5].

'Poor lass,' Marjorie Doors muttered. 'It's an evil world out there.' As she spoke, her knitting needles flew like pistons on a steam train. No one knew what she was knitting. Some said that even Marjorie didn't know what she was knitting.

Little Minnie Cooper blinked. 'It's pretty evil out here,' she said. 'This coffee's like poison.' She shuddered. She did a lot of that. She was just a shivery sort of woman.

They stared gloomily at the glittering glass tower. 'Loaf's Tower,' Edna said. 'Now *that's* an evil place, if you ask me.' She tapped the table with a yellow and horny nail. 'Nobody knows what goes on in there.'

'Arfur Loaf knows what goes on in there,' Minnie reminded her. 'It's his tower.'

---

5 A boxer? I mean a person who punches other people and gets punched for fun. I do NOT mean a boxer dog, which doesn't have a boxer's arms ... or any sort of arms.

Edna Crudge cringed. 'Well, yes, Arfur Loaf knows...'

'And his twisted assistant with the black eyepatch, Igon, *he* knows what goes on,' Marjorie reminded her.

Edna was breathing heavily through her nose – like a horse. 'Yes-s-s, Igon knows...'

'And the workers that work there, *they* know, even if they aren't allowed to say,' Minnie reminded her.

Edna had red spots in her grey cheeks now and her voice was shrill. 'All *right*, Minnie. When I say *no one knows*, I mean no *normal* people don't know.'

Marjorie sniffed. 'She means *she* don't know,' she told little Minnie. 'And if there's one thing Edna Crudge can't stand, it's not knowing.'

Edna gripped her coffee cup in her talons till it could have cracked. 'What I'm saying *is* ... *we* don't know what goes on in there.'

Minnie looked at Marjorie. Marjorie looked at Minnie. 'Yes, Edna, we *know* that's what you're saying,' Minnie added. 'But *why* are you saying it?'

Edna was confused. She hated being confused as much as she hated not knowing something. Suddenly, she dropped the cup. Luckily it was empty. 'Look,' she croaked. 'It's that Igon .... Evil Arfur Evil Loaf's evil assistant.'

The man in black wore a black eyepatch. He turned his eye left then right as he left the great glass doors of the great glass tower. He set off at a shambling trot towards the High Street. 'Follow him, Minnie,' Edna Crudge ordered. 'See where he's going.'

Minnie's mouth fell open; her false teeth clattered.

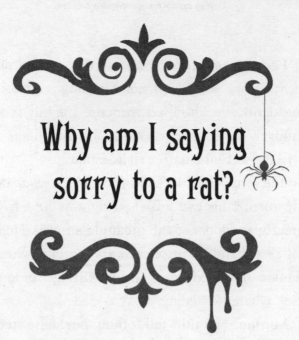

Why am I saying
sorry to a rat?

I n the caverns and the canyons of the old town there were places where the sun was afraid to shine. Dank Alley was such a place.

You won't find it on any town map. 'Dank Alley' was chalked on the wall at the entrance. Maybe it was a joke.

The tall walls of the alley were of warped wood and soot-stained stone. The cobbles glowed with their own green light and were slippery under the soles of the boy's trainers. He was a small boy, thin as rainwater and with a moon-pale, moon-hard face.

The narrow strip of watery sky was all that lit the black wooden walls. Crows were thrown across the sky like black confetti, gap-feathered and wailing like the wind through the planks.

Only a fool would walk into Dank Alley alone. Alone ... apart from the laughing rats that squeaked their joy[6].

Boy splashed through the puddles. He stopped and rested his foot on a rat that was too slow to get out of his way. It squawked as loud as the crows overhead and slithered away with a trodden tail.

'Sorr-ee,' the thief said, then laughed. 'Sorry? Why am I saying sorry to a rat?'

He peered at the doors, but they were cobwebbed shut and had no sign to say what lay behind. He pushed further into the gloom. At last, he came across a sign under a glowing gas lamp.

Once it had been richly painted, red with golden letters. Once it had said *Wiggott's Wonderful Waxworld*. Underneath, even fainter writing said *Deliveries – Knock three times*.

Knock-knock. Nothing. His knuckles sank into the rotting wood of the ancient door.

---

6 You get the picture? Right, that's enough. Let's get on with the story.

Knock-knock-knock. 'That's five,' a voice croaked from inside. 'I never answer the door to five knocks. Only three knocks.'

Knock-knock-knock.

'That's eight.'

'I can't un-knock your door, can I? I can't do *three* now I've done *eight*,' the boy complained.

'That's your problem,' the voice creaked. It sounded as ancient as the door.

'Fine,' Boy shouted, and his voice echoed down the alley loud enough to scare the crows. 'Fine. You don't get your *present*. I'll take it *back*, shall I?'

The door groaned open. In the dim light of the faded grey sky he could only see a faded grey eye. A clawed hand reached out with a dirty handkerchief and rubbed at the door. 'There you go. I rubbed out the eight knocks,' the man's voice said. 'Try again.'

The man was mad. The alley was mad. The world was mad. Mad as a rat with a trodden tail.

I've only got one seat on me bike

The boy knocked three times. The door opened swifter than a butterfly's wing. The caretaker's face was as thin as his body and still thinner wisps of hair clung to his shining head. Picture a pink egg with hair and you can picture his head. 'You knocked?' he asked.

'You know I did,' the boy cried.

'No need to shout. I am not deaf, you know. Fifty pence,' he said.

'You what?'

'It's *you* that's deaf. Fifty pence to enter here. There's nothing free.'

'I don't want to enter your smelly place. . .'

The door began to close. Then the boy heard a crackle and a voice crinkle on a radio from the far end of Dank Alley. 'Calling Constable Elloe,' the voice said. 'The boy ran into Dank Alley. Pursue and apprehend. Roger.'

'My name's not Roger. I'm Police Constable L.O. Elloe[7]. On the beat.'

'Elloe. . .'

Hello?'

'Listen, Elloe. We have tracked the thief on CCTV. . .'

'BBC TV?'

'No. CC, see?'

'CCC?'

'Listen, Elloe. The thief was seen entering Dank Alley. It is a dead-end street. He is trapped. You are the nearest patrol. Do you have your fast-response vehicle?' the radio voice asked.

'I've got me bike,' the policeman said proudly and patted the saddle. His bushy brows were too old for his young face.

'Enter the alley. Apprehend the thief, handcuff him and bring him to the station.'

---

7 You may think you can see the dreadful jokes that will follow with a name like 'L.O. Elloe.' Well, there will be no more pitiful puns like that in this twisting tale. Trust me.

'You want me to put him on a train?'

'Not the *railway* station. The *police* station, Elloe.'

'Hello? I've only got one seat on me bike. It's not a tandem, you know.'

'There is no patrol car to assist. The whole of Wildpool police force is searching for the missing girl. But that thief's a slippery character. He's made the steal of the century.'

'What's he stolen?' Elloe asked.

'We don't know yet. Just catch him and you'll be a hero on your first day on the force. Go, Elloe, go.'

'I can see a weedy boy down at the dark end of the alley, knocking at a door,' the policeman muttered. He crowed to himself, 'Go, Elloe, go.'

Are you daft or deaf?

Boy shivered in the doorway of Wiggott's Wonderful Waxworld. The policeman in the bright High Street, at the far end of Dank Alley, loomed through the gloom and looked twice as large as life. 'I just want this package to get to Mr Wiggott,' the boy said quickly to the shadowy figure behind the door.

'You said you didn't want to come into my *smelly* place,' the old man sniffed.

'But I want the money,' the boy burbled. 'I've got to deliver this to old Wiggott.'

'It's *Doctor* Wiggott to the likes of you. You want

his money? You'll just have to want, Sonny Jim. No one comes here calling my place smelly. Shove off.'

'But the policeman's coming. He'll arrest me and Dr Wiggott will be furious.'

A faint light from above made the watery eye of the old man glitter. 'You should have thought of that. Not my problem if Dr Wiggott gets upset with you.'

The door to Wiggott's Wonderful Waxworld was creaking closed. '*You*,' the boy cried. 'Wiggott will be furious with *you*, you old goat.' The boy looked around and saw nothing but wooden walls and rusting dustbins. There was no escape.

The door stopped. It was stuck. The old man muttered, 'Wiggott's wonderful warped doors,' and he grunted as he pulled with all the might of his weedy arms.

In the darkest corner of this dingy alley the boy's moon face glowed. PC Elloe saw the boy's face and shouted, 'Oi, boy. Stay there while I arrest you[8].' He gathered his bicycle in his right hand and began to wheel it steadily down the dim alley. Through puddles and past cobwebbed doors.

---

8 I know. I know. That's a stupid thing to shout. But you have to remember, PC Elloe is a stupid young copper. If he was a bit more stupid, he could be a chief constable in no time. Though Chief Constable Betterton Nunn may have had something to say about that.

'Shut . . . you daft door,' the caretaker cried.

The boy stared at the plodding policeman. A voice said, 'Inside the Waxworld.'

It felt like a voice in his head . . . or a voice from the top pocket of his hooded jacket. 'What?'

'Inside the door . . . Are you daft or deaf?' came the voice. A girl's voice with more metal than a brass bell.

'Who said that?'

'Never mind who said it. Just do it. Hide in the Waxworld. It's the only way to save yourself.'

As the old caretaker struggled to push the door shut, the boy pushed it open. He tumbled into the musty gloom. 'Here, what you doing?' the old man gasped.

'Shut up and close the door,' the voice from the boy's pocket said tiredly. 'Are you two sharing one brain cell?'

The boy and the old man pushed the door shut. *Thunk.*

Have you ANY idea how much fluff there is in your pocket?

'Now what?' the boy asked. It suddenly seemed as if he couldn't move without orders from the voice.

'Take me out,' came the order.

The boy stretched his bone-thin fingers into his pocket and pulled out the mobile phone. It glowed as amber as a traffic light[9]. He peered at it and saw the face of a girl staring back. A rather cross and

---

9 The MIDDLE bit of a traffic light, OBVIOUSLY. 'Amber' is the posh word for 'orange' . . . not green or red. Now let me get on with the story.

scowling face framed by pigtails like bell-ropes. Her eyes were the colour of tears. It was the face he'd glimpsed inside a glass case in Loaf Tower.

The face gave a tight smile. 'That's better. I can see where I am now. Have you ANY idea how much fluff there is in your pocket? Dis-*gus*-ting.'

'Who are you?' the boy asked.

The girl pulled a mocking face. '*You* should know. *You* stole me. I'm the face of the new phone. The most secret and valuable phone in the world. The *cleverest* phone too ... though I say it myself,' she explained. 'You're delivering me to Dr Wiggott so he can find out my secrets and make his fortune.'

'How did you know?' the boy gasped.

'I *told* you, I'm the cleverest phone in the world. And I hope he's paying you plenty because I'm priceless,' the girl said and smiled.

'A thousand pounds,' the boy murmured.

'That much!' the old man wailed. 'More than I make in a month.'

'That *little*,' the face on the phone laughed. 'Dr Wiggott is a bigger robber than the boy here. I'm worth a million,' she said.

The old man choked and spluttered. He stretched out a claw-hand towards the amber machine. 'I'll take you to Dr Wiggott at once,' he said.

The boy pulled his hand back. 'No you won't. I'll see him myself. I want the reward. I stole the phone.'

'I want the reward ... I know where Dr Wiggott's room is,' the caretaker argued.

The boy's pale, thin face turned suddenly sly. 'I bet you don't.'

'I do, you cheeky young whippersnapper. You just jump on the electric railway, get off at the right Waxworld display and walk through it. His office is at the back.'

'There are dozens of displays. Which display is Wiggott hiding behind?' the boy asked.

It was the old man's turn to look sly. 'Give me half of your one thousand pounds and I'll tell you.'

'I'll give you a hundred,' the boy offered. There was a hammering on the back door.

'You'll get nothing if that policeman catches you,' the phone said.

You have to get off some time

The caretaker groaned and called, 'Hang on, you'll have the door off its hinges.'

'Open up in the name of the law. I am Police Constable Lawrence Olivier Elloe and I demand you open up. I have reason to believe you are concealing a criminal thieverator inside your building,' the voice bawled.

'Don't open it,' the boy begged.

'Why not?'

'Because … err … because … err…'

'Because if he's caught you won't get your one hundred pounds,' the girl's voice from the phone reminded him.

'I can't lock out the law,' the caretaker said.

'No, but you can give us a chance to escape,' she said.

The caretaker nodded. He pressed a switch on the floor beside his foot. There was a rattle and a clatter, a clattle and a ratter, and a small train came into sight with the green glow of a lamp on the front. 'Climb in,' he ordered. A wooden locomotive was coupled to a four-seat carriage, the colour of rainbows.

The boy jumped into the cab as the train slowed. He sat down with a thump, pressed a pedal on the floor and the train rumbled forward. Ahead of him the track twisted sharply and vanished round a bend that was lit with faint blue light. He could make out a sign at the side of the track that said *Dracula's Castle*, with wax figures standing stone still. 'A vampire,' Boy hissed. 'I don't want the blood sucked from my neck.'

'No, no, no,' the girl's voice sighed. 'This is the *real* Dracula – Vlad Dracula, a duke of Romania in the 1400s. This is a scene from the true history where some visitors upset him. . .'

The train slowed to a halt. The boy stared at

the gruesome scene in front of him. 'What did Dracula do?'

'The visitors forgot to take off their hats when they entered his palace,' the phone voice said sadly.

'But what is this Duke Dracula doing to them?'

'He is nailing their hats onto their heads[10]. Want to get off here?' the girl asked, and her amber face smirked from the screen.

'No,' the boy said.

'You have to get off some time,' she reminded him, and her mouth seemed to shrug.

The boy turned and looked back. The caretaker was tugging at the back door to let in the policeman. 'Which scene do we get off?' the thief shouted over his shoulder.

The old man waved, 'Get off when you see the...' *Crash*. The outside door banged open and the caretaker's words were swallowed by the sound. At that moment the train gave a jerk and rolled forward around the blue-lit bend.

'Stop in the name of the law,' was the last thing he heard before he plunged onwards and out of sight.

---

10 Yes, Vlad Dracula really did that ... but don't try this at home.

Visited the Waxworld and were never seen again

The train creaked and stopped at the next scene. It showed a gloomy street lit by the sickly white-green light of a gas street lamp. The cobbles shone with slime, just like Dank Alley outside. The street was built of tumbling, black-brick houses with windows like empty eyes.

The boy peered at the sign. He read slowly. 'Burke and Hare – Edinburgh 1828?' He laughed. 'A couple of tramps. Not scary like Dracula.'

'Let me see them,' the girl on the phone ordered. The boy held her up and the light from her pale face lit the wax figures. Grim faces, grimy faces, glass eyes glinting greedily. Eyes that seemed to watch you wherever you stood.

The two figures had shaggy hair that spilled out from battered hats. The large one had bear hair as black as Arthur Loaf's and his face was just as fat. Their soot-stained hands grasped the handles of a wheelbarrow. It was covered with a filthy blanket and two boots stuck out from underneath. 'A body? They're carrying a dead body in a wheelbarrow? Why would they do that?'

'Wait ... I'll look them up on the internet,' the phone-girl snapped. The phone hummed quietly for a few moments. 'Ah ... I've discovered something. . .'

'If Dr Wiggott's room is behind one of these scenes,' the boy cut in, 'we'll have to try them all. May as well start here. It looks harmless.'

'But you need to look at this. . .' the girl began.

The boy was out of the carriage and onto the trackside. As he stood peering into the dim scene, the air in front of him seemed to shiver and tremble.

First he noticed the smell. The air was scented

with soot and gas mixed with horse manure and stale human bodies[11].

Then the sounds. The hissing of the gas lamp and the distant barking of dogs. Then the feel of the slippery cobbles and the cold, damp air on his skin. He gasped and whispered, 'It's so real... This museum must have been brilliant when it was open... I wonder why it closed.'

The voice from the phone was shrill and angry. 'I was trying to tell you. I've been on the internet. Wiggott's Waxworld had to close down – visitors started to disappear.'

The boy gave a snort. 'Disappear? What do you mean?'

'What part of the word *disappear* do you not understand? Vanished. Visited the Waxworld and were never seen again. Dis ... appeared.'

'Oh. All the visitors?'

'Only some of them,' the girl said. 'Only the ones who were stupid enough to step off the train.'

---

11 Disgusting, yes. But there are worse things ... like the smell of a boys' toilet in any school.

What's in the barrow?

The wheelbarrow creaked. One of the men seemed to give a small groan. His glassy eyes moved and fixed on the boy. The boy swallowed hard.

The men had been bent over the barrow and now they slowly stood up straight. Close up, the larger man looked a lot more like Arfur Loaf, with his thick black bear hair.

'Ohhhh, me back. I'm too old to be pushing barrows through the streets of Edinburgh at this time of night,' he said and stretched till the musty brown coat billowed with dust and the fleas fled. He kept his eyes on the boy. 'Here, boy, want to earn yourself a penny?' He had an Irish accent.

The boy's mouth hung open and he muttered, 'He spoke. The waxwork spoke.'

The voice of the girl in the phone hissed quietly. 'Wiggott's Waxworld closed down because visitors who stepped off the train disappeared. The police said they weren't ordinary waxworks. They were animatronics.'

'Animal who?' the boy whispered into the phone.

'Never mind. Robots. But the robots started to programme themselves. They had a life of their own – they started to live their evil lives.'

'So Dracula. . .?'

'Probably started nailing hats onto visitors who stepped into his scene,' the girl explained. The boy shivered, but before he could ask, the shabby figure spoke again.

'I asked if you wanted to earn a penny, boy.' His voice was rough and his breath smelled of blocked drains.

'Yes,' the boy said. He couldn't tell you why

he said that – why he agreed to help these villains[12].

'No,' the girl's voice said firmly. 'These are Burke and Hare – bodysnatchers.'

The black-hatted, brown-suited, red-faced man blinked. His round face had folds of fat that almost hid his small, bright eyes. 'Hurr-hurr. Hear that, Hare? He says *yes-no*.'

His small, grey-skinned, skinny friend chuckled. The little man with a narrow knife nose looked a lot like Igon, the evil assistant to Loaf. 'All you have to do is push the barrow, boy. Give us a rest. Mr Burke here will give you a penny and I'll give you a penny. Can't say fairer than that. Or do you want more? Is that it?'

'What's in the barrow?'

'Just the poor corpse of an old soldier that died tonight. There's no harm in the feller. How much do you want us to pay you?' little Hare asked. His ferret nose twitched.

The boy took a deep breath. 'I want to find the door that leads to Dr Wiggott.'

Burke looked at Hare. Hare looked at Burke.

---

12 We all do that. Our mouths move and say the words when our brains are saying the opposite. We seem to be in need of brain-training ... or train-braining even.

'We can do that, no trouble, lad. Just you get this barrow to Surgeon's Square and we'll pay you AND set you on the road to Dr Wiggle.' But as he said it his fingers were crossed.

Would your mother miss you?

The boy-thief slipped the phone into his top pocket, picked up the handles of the barrow and began to wheel it over the cobbles. 'I can't see where we're going,' the girl complained.

'I told you, we're going to Surgeon's Square. The house of Dr Knox. Turn left here,' the round-faced Burke said.

The body in the barrow was light enough, but the wheel was crooked and it was hard work keeping it from skidding into the dirt-filled gutter in the middle of the road. Rats munched in the muck and scuttered away as the boy rolled forward. 'But if he's dead, why are you taking him to a doctor?' he asked[13].

The boots of Burke and Hare squelched through the stinking puddles and the horse droppings. From time to time, a drably dressed man or woman wandered past and the men gave the passers-by a cheerful greeting. Everyone in Edinburgh seemed to know Burke and Hare ... but no one got too close to the barrow and the body. The two men shared a stone jar of drink and supped from it. They didn't offer the boy any.

'Dr Knox is not your common, fix-your-bad-belly or patch-up-your-knife-wound doctor. No, he's more important than that. He's a *surgeon*. Surely you've heard of him, boy?'

'Never.'

'And how long did you say you'd lived in Edinburgh?' Burke asked.

'I've just arrived,' the boy said and the reply made hollow-eyed Hare choke on the drink.

'No parents?' Burke went on, and his rough voice was suddenly honey smooth.

Boy invented a story that would explain how

13 That's a good question, don't you think? A very good question. What's the answer? Don't ask me. I haven't read this story yet.

he came to those savage, sooty, stench-filled streets. 'I've a mother . . . but she's not here. She's sick. She sends me out thieving to earn my food.'

'And what if you never came home, boy? Would your mother miss you? Would the law come looking for you?' Hare asked.

The boy shrugged. 'Nobody knows I'm here,' he said, and that was almost the truth. For the Master-Thief knew; the Master-Thief had sent him.

'Poor boy, poor wee lad,' Burke sighed. 'Never mind, Burke and Hare will take care of you.'

'As soon as I find Dr Wiggott's door, I'll be out of here.'

'Then we'll have to make sure you don't find it,' Hare said. He spoke so quietly only the sharp microphone of the girl in the phone picked it up. The phone began to hum softly as it went into action, searching.

Suddenly, Hare said cheerfully, 'But Dr Knox doesn't want to cure old Edwin in the barrow. Hah! Oh, no. He wants to cut him up!'

We're not bodysnatchers, are we?

'Cut him up!' the boy gasped. 'Dr Knox is a cannibal? He wants to eat the old man?'

Burke and Hare hooted with laughter, a sound as tuneful as two broken bassoons. 'No, no, no,' Hare explained. 'Dr Knox is a teacher. He shows his students how the body works by cutting one up. Always keen to get his hands on fresh bodies is Dr Knox.'

'Or get his knives into them,' Burke added and laughed again.

The boy saw the phone glow in his pocket and slipped the secret device out as he tried to balance the barrow with his other hand. 'What is it?'

'It's true,' the phone said softly. 'Dr Knox was a famous surgeon in Edinburgh in 1828. The law let him take bodies from the prisons and cut them apart. The trouble was, there weren't enough dead prisoners to work on. So he started buying corpses from bodysnatchers.'

'Bodysnatchers?' the boy cried out too loud.

'No, no, no,' Hare exclaimed. 'We're not bodysnatchers, are we, Burke? Tell the lad.'

'We're not, we're not, we're not,' Burke chuckled and wrapped an arm around the boy's shoulder. The smell made the boy feel a little sick. 'Bodysnatchers wait till a corpse is buried in the graveyard. Then they wait till it's dark and dig up the coffin.'

'They stick the corpse in a sack ... that's why they call them "sack-em-up men", you see?' Hare went on. 'Of course, that's against the law. It's shocking. It upsets the families when they come back with flowers to find an empty grave.'

'But *you* do it,' the boy argued.

'No, no, no,' Hare said. He gave a wide smile

that showed cracked and black-green teeth. 'Burke's dear wife Helen runs a boarding house, see?' The boy shook his head.

'Sometimes our guests die in their beds. Old Tom here died owing us four pounds, see?'

'I thought his name was Edwin?' the boy frowned.

'Thomas *Edwin* here died . . . we're just selling his body to get back what he owes us. He's happy with that, aren't you Tom?' Hare joked and shook the boot that stuck out from under the blanket[14].

The barrow rolled on and the streets grew lighter and cleaner, the houses finer and the smell sweeter. They were entering a richer part of town.

'But isn't it against the law?' the boy asked.

'Yes,' his phone moaned.

'No. . .' Burke began. Then he looked up and twitched. 'Oh, good evening, Constable Craig. How nice to see you.'

---

14 The body didn't answer. It ignored the question. That is a very rude thing to do. Always answer when someone asks you a question. Being dead at the time is no excuse.

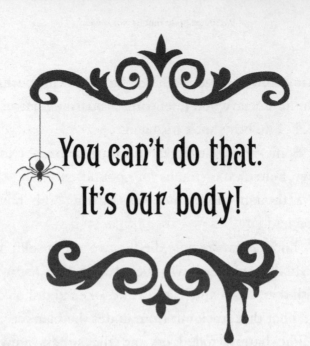

You can't do that.
It's our body!

The constable was a large man with a fat red face. Long grey side-whiskers flowed out from under his greasy top hat. He carried a lantern in one hand and a shiny black stick in the other. His face looked as hard as the stick. 'What have we here?' he asked.

'Where?' Burke asked and tried to make his round face as innocent as a baby.

'In the barrow, Mr Burke,' the constable said wearily.

The little eyes scanned the street. He caught sight of the boy and the barrow as if for the first time. 'Oh, *that* barrow!' he cried. 'Never seen it in my life. Have you ever seen that barrow, Hare?'

'Never,' his thin friend agreed. 'We were just taking a walk – looking for a quiet tavern, weren't we, Burke?'

The constable turned his gaze on the boy. 'You're new. So, what's your name?'

'I don't have one.'

The constable sighed. 'Everybody has a name. What does your mother call you?'

He shrugged. 'The Master just calls me *Boy*[15].'

Constable Craig blew out his cheeks. 'That's what we'll have to put on your gravestone. Here lies the body of Boy.'

'My gravestone?'

'Oh yes. Do I have to explain? I can see you have a body in the barrow. You are a bodysnatcher and the punishment for bodysnatching is hanging.' He placed a hand on Boy's shoulder. 'I arrest you in the name of the law. Bring that barrow along to the lock-up. You'll go in front of the judge tomorrow and they'll let you see a priest before they hang you.'

'You can't do that,' the boy gasped.

15 Sad, yes. But not as sad as being called 'Mushroom' ... or 'Pig's Bum' ... or 'Sweetie Pie'.

'Oh yes he can,' the girl's voice said from his pocket. 'It says here there were over two hundred reasons to hang someone in the early 1800s.'

'Shut up.'

'Don't you tell me to shut up,' the constable barked and waved his stick under the boy's nose.

'I was only pushing the barrow,' Boy said fiercely and squirmed under the iron grip of the law officer.

'Hah! That's what they all say. You were taking this illegal corpse to Dr Knox in Surgeon's Square to sell for seven pounds and ten shillings. I am confiscating this body ... as soon as I lock you up for the night.

'You can't do that. It's our body!' Burke wailed.

There was silence. Boy and the constable and Hare – even the street rats – turned to look at him.

He says it wasn't his fault – what a laugh

'No, it's not *our* body,' Hare said quickly and gave his friend Burke a sharp jab in the ribs with his needle elbow. 'It's not our body at all.'

The constable looked at them. He spoke slowly. 'It is the *boy's* body. I know that because you told me so. Now, if you feel sorry for this poor nameless lad, you could buy his freedom. Five pounds.'

'One pound,' Hare said quickly.

'Three.'

'Two.'

'Two golden guineas and it's a deal,' the constable agreed. Burke handed over two coins from a purse in his pocket. 'On your way ... and don't let me catch you again. Five pounds next time.' He jingled the two coins in his fat fist. 'This will go to charity. To the Chimney Sweep Boys' Rescue fund. Those little lads will be so-o-o happy when I give them this.'

'Yeah, right,' the phone-girl said.

The constable grabbed Boy by the front of his jacket. 'What did you say?'

'Delight,' Boy said quickly. 'A delight to give money to those poor boys.'

The constable nodded, satisfied. The man had a leather strap on his heavy black stick. He slipped the strap over his wrist and swung it like a windmill as he plodded on down the street.

Hare turned his pinched face towards Boy. 'Two pounds and two shillings you cost us. Two pounds and two shillings.'

The boy shook his head. 'It wasn't my fault.'

Hare snorted, 'Hear that, Burke? He says it wasn't his fault. What a laugh.'

'Hurr! Hurr!' Burke laughed.

Hare brought his face close to the boy's. 'You're a thief, aren't you?'

Boy nodded.

'And what is the first rule of thieving?'

Boy closed his eyes and said quietly, 'Don't get caught.'

'And what did you do, eh? What...' he said and poked Boy's shoulder with each word, 'did ... you ... do?'

'But...'

'You got caught. You owe us two pounds and two shillings. How are you going to pay us?'

'Deliver this body,' Boy sighed.

'Oh, no,' Hare breathed. 'Delivering bodies is only worth a couple of shillings. You won't have paid us back till you've delivered TWENTY bodies[16].'

'Hurr! Hurr!' Burke chuckled. 'That'll keep you busy for months. Hurr.'

---

16 They say 'Crime doesn't pay.' That's not always true. What they should say is, 'A crime like delivering dead bodies doesn't pay very well ... so don't do it.' Unless you are an undertaker, of course.

I have to find that door…

Little William Hare supped from the stone jar and walked ahead of Boy. The road was smooth and clean now. A wooden post said *Surgeon Square* and he led the way into a street of fine stone houses with pillared porches and shiny doors that glinted in the powerful gaslights. Spiked iron railings in rows kept out the dogs and the burglars.

Brass plates on gateposts told visitors who lived there, and Boy stopped at the one that said *Dr Knox – Surgeon to the King.*

Burke was following and placed a fat hand in

the boy's back. 'Not here, lad, the constables will arrest you.'

When Boy looked puzzled, Hare went on: 'The *back* door, laddie. We do our deals in darkness[17].'

The alley that led to the back gates in Dr Knox's row was as gloom-filled as a rain cloud. Cats chased rats through the shadows and dogs chased the cats. *Squeak, yowl, bark, creak* … the creak was the barrow wheel.

Hare pushed open a gate in a high back wall and walked up the back path to a door that was smaller and more dull than the grand one at the front. He pulled a rope and a bell jangled deep inside the house. In fifteen barks of a distant dog, the door opened slowly. A man stood there with a candle.

A man so tall he had to stoop in the doorway. 'What can I do for you?' he asked in a smooth voice.

'We've a nice fresh body for you, Dr Knox. Died early tonight,' Hare said and twisted his hands together as if he were washing them.

'Let me see,' the surgeon said and stepped

---

17 I once sold a friend a broken torch. He said, 'This torch is broken' and I said, 'I do my deals in darkness.' He wasn't my friend for long. Just thought I'd mention that. Bet you're glad I did.

forward. He reached for the blanket but the candle lit its filth and he stopped. 'Pull back the blanket.'

Burke reached forward. Boy turned away. He didn't want to watch or hear. He wandered back to the gate into the alley and chewed his lip with worry. 'How did I get into this?' he moaned. The phone glowed amber in his pocket.

'You stepped off the train at Wiggott's,' the girl reminded him.

'I have to find that door ... and sell you to Dr Wiggott. Burke and Hare can help me,' he said.

'You think so?' the girl asked. 'There's something you need to know about Burke and Hare.'

'They said they knew where to find Wiggott's room,' the boy hissed.

'And you believed them? Are you really that stupid?'

'I'm cleverer than a mobile phone. You're the stupid one,' he snapped.

There was a very faint click. The phone went dark and silent. Boy was alone.

You want me to sleep in a dead man's bed?

The boy heard Burke and Hare struggle with something before the sounds were muffled into silence as they carried it into the house. A minute later they were back in the yard jingling coins and laughing. 'It's down to the Grassmarket Tavern for a few pints of gin and some of Mrs McDonald's mutton stew,' Hare said.

'Hurr! Hurr! Gin and stew. I likes that,' Burke agreed.

'You have to show me Dr Wiggott's door first,' Boy reminded them as they hurried from the new town towards the slimy streets of West Port.

Hare threw his hands in the air. 'I'd love to, laddie, but we can't let you out of our sight till we get the two guineas you owe us.' The men slithered off into the smoky gloom where coal fires dropped their soot on to everyone in the street. It stung Boy's nose and made him sneeze.

'You promised,' he said running after the men.

'I promised,' Hare said, '*before* you were stupid enough to get yourself caught.' He stopped suddenly. 'But you're a good lad, so I'll tell you what I'll do. I'll buy you a plate of Mrs McDonald's stew ... and a pint of gin to wash it down. And that's not all ... me and Burke will give you a bed for the night at Mrs Burke's lodging house.'

'Hurr! Hurr!' Burke nodded. 'Old Tom won't be needing it any more. Hurr!'

'You want me to sleep in a dead man's bed?' Boy gasped.

'It's not like you have to *share* it with him ... though his coffin's in the room ready for the funeral tomorrow,' Hare said, shuffling on.

'But you've just taken his body to Dr Knox,' Boy argued.

'That's right. So we've filled the coffin with

tree bark and that's what they'll bury tomorrow,' the thin man explained[18].

'Hurr! It'll be funny if them bodysnatchers go digging it up, hurr!' Burke laughed.

He was still laughing when they reached the door to the Grassmarket Tavern. The noise from the doorway made the gaslamps tremble outside. The air was foggy with tobacco smoke from a hundred clay pipes. A fiddler played a tune as fast as a sparrow's wing and twenty men and women danced a jig in the hot crowded room. Their boots clattered on the sawdust floor and they screamed as they whirled around.

Burke shouted to a woman in a stained red dress, 'Three plates of your best stew, Mrs McDonald. And three jars of gin.'

'I don't drink gin,' Boy shouted.

Burke nodded. 'Hurr! Give the boy a glass of laudanum then.'

'What's laudanum?' he asked, as a pot of murky liquid was pushed into his hand. He shouted into his top pocket. 'What's laudanum?' But the phone-girl sulked silently. He was thirsty. He stared into the pot.

---

18 Burying bark instead of a body. Something ELSE you mustn't do. It's a grave crime.

Why would you get caught?

Boy looked at the dish that sat on the table in front of him. Lumps of fat were swimming in warm water[19]. He pushed the plate away. Burke snatched it and with five scoops of his wooden spoon he emptied it. 'Lovely,' he said and wiped his mouth on his sleeve. 'Now, lad, try your laudanum,' he shouted over the deafening din of the dancers.

Boy sniffed at the drink and it smelled of medicine. He sipped it and it was as bitter as lemons. The heat was making him thirsty, so he

---

19 When I say 'swimming', I don't mean they were doing the breaststroke or the crawl. They just floated there like dead jellyfish ... and twice as deadly.

swallowed the cup in two gulps. He didn't turn his head, but his view of the room shifted. The dancers twirled faster, the fiddle sounded like the wail of a dying penguin. The pipe smoke grew thicker. And thicker. He'd never felt so tired.

Boy was asleep before his face fell forward into the empty stew bowl. He didn't see Burke and Hare drink and dance. Midnight struck on the Grassmarket clock, and the customers from the tavern swayed and swooped and whooped their way home.

He didn't feel the hard hands of Burke grab him under the arms or Hare's nimble fingers pick up his feet. The two men carried him to the barrow and dumped him in. They took turns at wheeling him down the darkly rutted and ratted alleys to Mrs Burke's house.

'What have we here?' Mrs Burke asked her husband. She was a large woman with two chins where most of us have one. She was very like Lady Greystone in the outside world of Wildpool.

'A young villain to do our work for us. We'll send him to push the bodies to Dr Knox. He'll bring the money back to us,' Hare explained. 'That way we don't get caught.'

'Why would you get caught?' Mrs Burke said, and her large body wobbled with a shiver at the very idea.

'We were stopped by Constable Craig tonight,' Burke said.

'But you bribed your way out of the noose on the gallows,' the woman said. Her red face had turned pale.

'We did,' Burke nodded, 'but it cost us two guineas. Next time it might be one of the honest constables that stops us. Then where would we be?'

'Dangling from the gallows today ... being cut to pieces by Dr Knox tomorrow,' Mrs Burke said. 'Throw the lad in old Jamie's room.'

'Jamie? I thought his name was Tom? Hurr!' Hare said.

The woman shrugged her huge shoulders. 'Who cares? He was a homeless old man. We gave him a comfy last bed and a happy end. Put the boy on his straw.'

Burke and Hare dragged the boy's sleeping

body towards the bedroom. They edged around the coffin on the table. They hadn't noticed something slip out of Boy's top pocket and lie in the straw on the floor of the kitchen.

The thing gave a small bleep and glowed a soft amber.

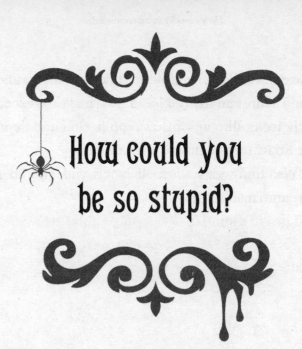

How could you be so stupid?

The girl's face on the phone folded into a frown. 'Oh, Boy,' she sighed. 'Such a clever thief – how could you be so stupid?'

Then the face began to shimmer and wobble. Her brainpower was crackling and fading. She began to have flashes of memory about how she arrived here.

Back in the outside world of Wildpool, about thirty or forty minutes before, she had felt a shock of electric as her battery switched on and she awoke. A large man with the hair of a bear had been staring at her screen and smiling proudly. 'Lady Greystoke, let me show you the world's most amazing phone ... the infinit-G.'

'It looks like any other mobile phone to me, Mr Loaf,' the woman replied, frowning.

'Wait and see, Lady Greystoke, wait and see,' the large man said.

The girl's mind in the phone felt the electricity surge through her and began to hum. She operated herself. She 'thought' the words. *Loaf. Phone. infinit-G.* Then *Search.*

In an instant, the words unwound in her head...

ARFUR LOAF - FACTORY OWNER

Arfur Loaf's father always said the old saying was true: ''alf a loaf is better than none.' So he named his son Arfur and said, 'Arfur Loaf is better than anyone in the world.' (Sadly, his father was not good at spelling.)

Arfur grew up believing that he was the best. As he made millions with new inventions, he made a lot of enemies. But his enemies say Loaf never invented a thing - he simply stole the best ideas of other inventors.

Loaf's assistant, the one-eyed weed known as Igon, may have invented the world's greatest phone, the infinit-G. But Arfur Loaf planned to make those very special phones and sell them to the rich.

Latest update: The Loaf Company has moved into Loaf Tower in Wildpool, where the first infinit-G phone will be tested and shown to the richest people in the land.

No one knows when this will happen as it is a secret plan by a secret man in a secret tower made with flour power. (Loaf ... flour ... geddit?)

The girl had turned her camera eye back to Arfur Loaf as he stood by a glass case. There seemed to be a girl lying in the case. A girl with a face she knew as well as her own...

Loaf was a fine figure of a man. His shoulders

were as wide as a sumo wrestler's, and his shiny dark hair swept back from his ugly face and a smile of crooked teeth.

The girl saw a small man with an eyepatch standing behind Arfur Loaf and looking worried. 'That'll be Igon,' she decided.

She felt all eyes in the room were on her. Diamond-hard eyes, cross-eyes of a man in a white coat and a single worried eye. They were waiting for her to show her power. The girl-phone was ready.

So she did not expect what happened next.

A cup of tea was placed in front of her[20]. She was about to be stolen.

20 This is better than placing a mobile phone IN a cup of tea. Don't ever try that. You get a wet phone and an even wetter hand when you start to use it.

Chimpanzees don't have tails

F ive minutes after the phone theft, at the café opposite Loaf Tower, the Ladies Who Crunch had watched Boy leave the building.

Ten minutes after that, Minnie Cooper spied the man with the eyepatch limp down the High Street and followed him just as Edna Crudge had ordered. Every time he turned to look back she ducked into a shop doorway, fast as a sloth with sore toes.

Igon reached a building the colour of mouldy bread. It had a blue lamp over the door and the glass had white writing that spelled out *Police*. Igon stepped inside.

'Ooooh,' Minnie moaned to herself. Minnie spent a lot of time talking to herself. 'What do I do now, Edna?'

'My name's not Edna,' a passing street sweeper snapped at her.

The real Edna Crudge was back at the café and she didn't reply. She wouldn't and couldn't. She didn't even hear the question. Minnie had to decide for herself. She decided to enter the police station.

Igon, the man in black, was standing at a counter talking to the boys in blue[21].

'My employer, Arfur Loaf, wishes to make a complaint,' Igon was saying. His voice creaked like a rusted gate on a rusted hinge in a rusted wall by a rusted house.

The grey-haired policeman with a grey moustache had three white stripes on the arm of his blue jacket. He sucked the tip of his pencil. That would be what turned his moustache grey. 'Half . . . a . . . loaf. . .' he wrote. 'You know what they say: "Half a loaf is better than none."'

---

21 The Wildpool police uniforms were black and blue. A bit like my Uncle Edward when he fell down a hundred and one concrete steps. 'Ooooof,' you gasp. 'Horrible.' But don't worry, the steps weren't damaged at all.

'Arfur . . . like King Arfur . . . the famous leader of the Knights of the Round Table,' Igon said.

'There's one of them down at the Blue Bell pub,' the police sergeant said.

'A knight? In the Blue Bell?' Igon blinked . . . or it could have been a wink.

'No. A round table.'

Igon blew out his cheeks. 'Listen, I am not supposed to tell you this, but he has had a mobile phone stolen. . .'

'No problem. There's a shop next door. He can easily get a new one.' The policeman smiled a moustache-bending smile.

'This is a very special mobile phone. The only one in the world. Mr Loaf phoned and reported something stolen twenty minutes ago. He even described the boy who stole it.'

The sergeant nodded wisely. 'Ah, yes, I took the call myself. And I told Mr Loafer our constable PC L.O. Elloe followed the suspect and cornered him. We'll have him locked away in two shakes of a chimpanzee's tail.'

'Chimpanzees don't have tails,' Igon argued.

The sergeant looked glum. 'I know. And we

don't have the boy-thief. Not exactly. But, as I say, Constable Elloe is on the case. That's the best we can do.'

'This Constable Elloe ... is he your best officer?'

'No. He's our worst. I'm afraid all the good ones are out looking for this missing girl.' The policeman leaned forward. 'Between me and you, your Mr Loafer's phone could be gone a very long time.'

Are you trying to put us out of a job?

'I believe Mr Loaf will offer a thousand pound reward for its return,' Igon said.

'Ooooh,' Minnie gasped. 'I could do with a thousand pounds,' she said to herself. 'What do I want with a thousand pounds?' she asked herself. 'To keep me warm next winter,' she replied. Minnie Cooper shrank into a corner of the police station and pretended to read the 'Wanted' notices.

Igon stamped again and raged ... as well as any voice, which creaks like a see-saw *can* rage. 'So you are making no attempt to find Mr Loaf's precious phone?'

'Constable Elloe is doing his best. . .'

'How good is his best?'

The sergeant spread his hands, helpless. 'Not very good. But his dad is a chief inspector and Constable Elloe is very good at teaching children to ride their bicycles safely.'

'But not very good at finding smartphone thieves?'

'Depends how smart the phone thieves are. But I'd say he's *very* good at finding them. He's found this one already. He may just have a problem arresting the rascals when he finds them.'

Igon jabbed the counter with a white finger with every word he said: 'Then – I – will – have – to – arrest – the – thief – my – self.'

The sergeant's moustache glowed red in the light of his red and angry cheeks. 'We can't have that, we can't have that. Are you trying to put us out of a job?'

'Yes,' Igon said.

The sergeant sighed. 'Very well, you'll find Constable Elloe tracking the suspect down at Wiggott's Wonderful Waxworld, on the High Street.'

'Thank you,' Igon said[22]. 'But I already knew that. I was hoping your pathetic policeman would have made an arrest by now and saved me the trouble.'

Igon limped to the door. He passed an elderly lady in a colourless coat and didn't notice her. Minnie turned to follow. Suddenly the police sergeant said, 'And what can I do for you, madam? Sorry to keep you waiting.'

Minnie was flustered. Wouldn't you be? She could not turn back and say, 'I was following that man who just walked out ... now push off.' Instead she said, 'I've lost my purse.'

'Colour?' the sergeant said, sucking his pencil and turning to a clean sheet of paper.

'Ginger.'

'Ginger? A ginger purse?'

'Purse?' Minnie giggled. 'I meant to say puss. My ginger cat. And I just saw him walk down the street. Have to hurry,' she said, backing towards the door. 'It has all my money inside.'

'Your puss?'

'My purse. Bye.' And she left the policeman snapping his pencil.

22 It always pays to be polite to policemen. There is an old saying: 'If you want to know the time, ask a policeman.' Practise politeness. You never know when you may need to know the time.

Ooooh, you'd better come in then

Igon wandered down the front of Wildpool High Street looking for Wiggott's Wonderful Waxworld. He passed dingy shops that sold walking sticks or woodworm cures, crumbly cakes and broken biscuits, pets like puppies, parrots and Polish piglets, clothes, both new and old, from worn waistcoats and badged blazers to sky-red scarlet skirts and saffron shirts and stained shorts. He could buy mutton and buttons or shutters or butter. But he couldn't find a Wonderful Waxworld.

The old front of Wiggott's fantastic fun-palace

was boarded up now and spiders lived in peace behind the old gold doors.

But Minnie Cooper knew just where to go to find a way inside. She headed down the damp back lane that ran *behind* the street of shops. She would get to the back door of Wiggott's and be waiting for the eyepatched evil assistant to arrive. She turned down the lane known as Dank Alley.

The puddled path was home to rats and slimier than jellied eels. Minnie trembled, Minnie shivered, Minnie moaned. 'I have to do it, I have to find the phone. A thousand pound reward. I'll buy a new blue coat and still have change to buy a hat,' she said to herself. 'Yes, a woman needs a hat,' she agreed with herself. 'A purple one.'

The sun was hazy in the morning sky, but its bright beams never shone in Dank Alley[23]. Minnie stepped into the shade and shuffled past the doors, which were barred and chained and padlocked shut. But a small door was set inside the large doors.

She saw a policeman's bicycle propped up

23 The boy-thief is in Burke and Hare's Edinburgh, asleep at night, as you know. How come it's still morning in Wildpool? I'm glad you asked. Time inside the Waxworlds is different. You can live a year inside a Waxworld and then step out – only a minute has passed in the outside world. How is that? It's like a dream. I will say no more.

against the wooden wall. She knew it was a policeman's bicycle because the label on the saddle said *Police property – Do not steal*. Minnie peered at a sign on the door. Once it had been burning red with golden letters. The letters had said *Wiggott's Wonderful Waxworld*. Underneath, white writing said *Deliveries – Knock three times*.

Knock, knock, knock!

Minnie pulled her coat around her and pushed some courage into her heart. The warped door groaned as someone struggled to open it. Finally, it flew open and the old caretaker peered out. 'Good afternoon, Miss Cooper,' he said.

'Good afternoon, Mr Crudge. Your Edna sent me along.'

The old man's sunken face almost sank out of sight. 'Edna? Our Edna sent you? Ooooh, you'd better come in then.'

Minnie stepped inside and a policeman in a bright-buttoned uniform blinked at her. She thought he looked just about old enough to be at school ... just about. His round and simple face was wide-eyed and wary. His eyes looked scared under the bushy brows.

'Good afternoon. You must be Constable Elloe,' she said politely.

'Constable L.O. Elloe at your service,' he replied and saluted.

'Hello, L.O. Elloe,' she said and closed the door to shut them in near darkness.

Heart of gold,
that man

Back in the Burke and Hare Waxworld, the girl in the phone lay in the straw of Mrs Burke's lodging house and glowed into life again. 'Not so clever now, are you, Boy?' she said, and whirred and searched.

She muttered, 'Laudanum. A sleeping drug. Hmmmm. How will you get out of this, Boy?'

In the next room, Boy woke slowly and his head felt as if he were wearing a knight's helmet. It was heavy and sounds seemed to jangle around. He groaned. The door to the bedroom swung open and a large woman blocked the light. 'You're awake then, lad? I've just boiled a pan of water. Want some tea for breakfast?'

'Urrrr,' Boy replied and tried to nod his heavy head. He struggled to his feet and swayed. Then he crashed against the doorpost before he collapsed onto a bench at the kitchen table. The coffin had gone in the night. Six men in black had carried it off.

The tea was sweet and the fresh bread the woman offered him had some odd crunchy bits, but he was hungry enough to eat them[24]. The woman smiled broadly and sat opposite him. 'It's so good to have you here,' she sighed.

'Is it?'

'Oh, yes. Hare and my husband are a bit rough at times ... but they have hearts of gold ... pure gold.'

'Really?'

'They offered a homeless child a bed, didn't they? You ARE homeless aren't you?'

'I suppose so.'

'Would you like honey on that bread? You need to build up your strength,' she said as she

---

24 The crunchy bits were probably little insects that had been living in the flour before it was cooked. Don't feel sorry for Boy. Feel sorry for the beetles he breakfasted on.

spooned honey onto his bread. 'It's sad when a boy has no mother to care for him. I suppose I could be like a mother to you. Would you like that?'

His mouth was full of honeyed bread, so he just nodded and looked into her crinkling, smiling eyes.

'I could even be your best friend. You're a stranger in Edinburgh, aren't you?' He nodded again. 'And no one knows you're here?'

Boy shook his head and said, 'Mr Hare asked me that last night.'

Mrs Burke nodded. 'Heart of gold, that man. He would hear you're alone and want to take you under his wing like the great golden goose that he is.'

Boy frowned. 'I need to get out. Out of Edinburgh – back to Dank Alley. Mr Burke and Mr Hare promised to tell me where I'd find Dr Wiggott's door . . . but they broke their promise.'

Mrs Burke's large chest heaved. 'Stay tonight. Stay one more night and tomorrow I will show you the way to Dr Waggott's door. I know it like my own front door. You trust me, don't you?' Boy nodded and she went on: 'I'm off to do some shopping. I'll make you a fine meal tonight,' she said, rising and picking up a basket. 'Have a rest.'

As she sailed through the door like a galleon, Boy heard the bleep of a phone alarm.

Now do you believe me?

Boy's hand reached for his top pocket. It was empty. 'Over here,' said the girl's voice, and the amber light flashed bright from the straw by the door.

'You are speaking to me again, then?' he asked as he picked up the machine and blew away the straw dust and mouse droppings. 'You've stopped sulking?'

'Only because you'll die if I don't,' the girl said quietly.

'Huh, I'm doing fine,' Boy snorted. 'I have found a friend and I'll be out of this weird world tomorrow morning.'

The girl's face appeared on the screen and it looked pitying. 'You will be out of here tonight . . . in the wheelbarrow . . . and by morning Dr Knox will be cutting you up. Now will you listen?'

'Mrs Burke is a lovely woman. She wouldn't let that happen to me. I don't believe you[25],' Boy said, and he felt his face burn with anger.

The girl shook her head slowly. 'You don't deserve my help, you fool. But I was lying here last night. I recorded what went on in the room after they drugged you to sleep.'

The boy shook his head. 'That laudanum wasn't a drug,' he argued. He pushed the phone in his pocket and stepped over to the door. 'I can leave any time I want,' he muttered. He lifted the latch. The door was locked.

He stumbled over to the back door. It was locked. None of the windows opened. 'Why's she locked me in?' he groaned. The girl stayed silent. 'I have to find Dr Wiggott and get my money.'

The girl stayed silent. He pulled the phone from his pocket and looked at the screen. Her face was gone. There was just a printed page. He read the title: **'BODYSNATCHERS'**.

---

25 People SAY that don't they? 'I don't believe you.' What they really mean is 'I don't WANT to believe you.'

Then the words 'Burke and Hare' caught his eye. He read their chilling history.

Burke and Hare are the most famous names in bodysnatching ... yet they weren't. They never dug up a single body from a grave. They just sold the bodies of poor people that had died in Mrs Burke's lodging house. They spent the money in the local taverns and needed more. So they started inviting people to stay in their house. Then they killed them and sold their bodies to Dr Knox. Burke and Hare weren't bodysnatchers — they were killers.

The girl's face appeared again. 'Now do you believe me?'

The boy frowned. 'You're the world's cleverest machine. You could have made that up. I don't believe Mrs Burke wants me to help her to kill people.'

The phone sighed. 'She doesn't, stupid. Watch this ... did I make this recording up?'

And the screen faded to a video showing a dirty lamp-lit room with three people sitting around a table. Mrs Burke's room. The people began to speak. . .

So you'll only need
three chops for dinner

The picture was so clear Boy felt he could reach out and touch the three people. They were Burke, Hare and Mrs Burke and they were sitting at the same table he sat at now. The oil lamp flickered and gave their faces a ghastly low glow like devils.

Mrs Burke said, 'Throw the lad in old Jamie's room.'

'Jamie? I thought his name was Tom? Hurr!' Burke said.

'Who cares? He was a homeless old man. We gave the old man a comfy last bed and a happy end. Put the boy on his straw. Now, where's my money? The old man owed me four pounds.'

Hare twisted his thin fingers, 'We only got six pounds from Dr Knox,' he whined[26].

Burke nodded, 'And we had to give two to Constable Craig.'

'And we spent another two in the Grassmarket Tavern,' Hare added. 'So I only have two pounds left.'

Mrs Burke held out a hand and her husband dropped the coins into it. 'That'll buy us four nice chops for dinner tonight,' she said. 'Porridge for breakfast and bread for dinner, tea and sugar and...'

'Gin, hurr, hurr,' Burke put in.

Mrs Burke turned to him and spat, 'Nothing left for your gin, Burke!'

'Ohhhh!' he wailed. 'I likes me gin.'

The woman leaned over the table and hissed, 'Then you'd better go out and earn more money. Do some work for a change ... a bit of thieving.'

Hare shook his head, 'Selling a body is quicker and makes us richer.'

---

26 YOU know this is a lie. He got seven pounds and ten shillings. But what did it matter? Mrs Burke lied to him and to Burke and to Boy, Burke lied to Mrs Burke and Boy and Hare and ... oh, everyone lied to everyone. Stop fussing and let me get on with the story.

The woman reached out and grabbed the front of his jacket, 'Then find an old beggar on the streets, offer him a hot meal and a warm bed . . . send him to sleep . . . and maybe he won't wake up in the morning, eh?'

Hare frowned. 'Dr Knox said he wasn't so happy with *old* people. He wanted some young-uns to practise on. He'll pay twice as much. Where will we find a young one?'

Mrs Burke gave a wide smile and looked towards the bedroom door. 'The boy.'

'Hurr! Hurr!' Burke chuckled. 'Now? While he's drugged? I sits on his chest and. . .'

'No!' the woman said sharply. 'Tomorrow afternoon. Keep him fresh. Deliver him tomorrow night before dinner . . . and after dark.'

Hare nodded. 'So you'll only need three chops for dinner tomorrow night.'

The three left the room and carried away the oil lamp. The screen faded to dark.

It's like you say, I have to save myself...

The boy sat in the gloom and stared at the cold ashes in the fireplace. The phone turned amber and the girl's face appeared. 'You'll leave here in the wheelbarrow,' she said quietly. 'I've helped you all I can. I may be the cleverest computer in the world, but I can't save you. Only you can save you, Boy.'

He nodded slowly. 'Thanks.' Suddenly he turned to her. 'What's your name?'

'What?'

'Your name. Do you have a name?'

The girl's face frowned. 'I think I had one

once.' She closed her eyes and whispered, 'Molly... I was a girl ... a real girl ... before I... I was called Molly.'

'Thank you, Molly. It's like you say, I have to save myself...'

The door rattled and a key turned in the lock. Mrs Burke bustled in, her wide face smiling but her eyes as cold as the ashes in her hearth. She locked the door behind her and placed her bunch of keys on a hook on her belt.

'Why lock the door?' Boy asked.

Mrs Burke emptied her basket onto the kitchen table and said, 'There's a lot of villains around in Edinburgh. They'd have your eyes before you could blink[27].' She put some packets on the table and some on a high shelf where the mice couldn't get them. 'Would you like a cup of tea?' she asked.

'How many chops did you buy?' he asked.

'Three,' she replied without thinking about what he's said.

Boy nodded, glanced at the girl on the phone then slipped her into his top pocket again. 'Can I have a hug?' he said suddenly. 'It's just...' he

---

27 Eye-thieves are a bit like schoolteachers. They have lots of pupils. Geddit? Sorry, no more bad jokes, I promise.

said, his voice breaking, 'I miss my mum ... and she always gave me a hug in the morning till she got too sick ... and you are just like my mum. Kind and ... and caring.'

The woman opened her arms and Boy stepped towards them. Her body smelled of Edinburgh's foul air. Her arms crushed him. He wriggled free.

'Thank you,' he said.

'Now, I'll light the fire and make the tea. We'll put a few drops of laudanum in it so you sleep this afternoon ... Mr Hare may want you wide awake to do a little job tonight,' she added quickly.

'With the wheelbarrow?' Boy asked.

'With the barrow, oh yes,' she murmured.

Boy turned away. There was a small smile on his face. There was a bunch of keys in his hand. Picking pockets was a skill he had learned in thief school.

Come here, you evil little thieving beggar!

Mrs Burke knelt in front of the hearth and began to sweep the cold ashes aside and lay twigs from a basket on the hearth. The boy tried to tiptoe towards the door, but the straw on the floor rustled.

'Where you going?' she asked, swinging round.

'Nowhere,' he told her. Every step betrayed him. Then the room was slowly filled with the sound of the wind whistling through cracks in the door and down the chimney. It took Boy a few moments to realise the noise was coming from the phone. He grinned. Clever Molly. She was making the wind noise to hide his footsteps and the sound of the keys as he slipped one into the lock.

The first key didn't turn. He pulled it out and tried a second one. 'I'll have to buy a newspaper,' Mrs Burke grumbled. 'I'll get Hare to block up that crack in the door.' By the time she turned around, Boy was back at the table. He nodded. The keys were behind his back. He ran them through his fingers and found the third one.

As soon as the woman reached for a tinder box to spark a light, he hurried back to the door. The wind howled louder. The key fitted and turned smoothly. He lifted the latch just as Mrs Burke turned again. Her eyes narrowed and in a moment she understood. Her hand clutched at her empty belt. 'Come here, you evil little thieving beggar[28]!' she roared.

'Run,' Molly cried. Boy didn't need her to tell him that. As Mrs Burke struggled to lift her heavy body, he sprang into the street and looked around.

'Lock the door behind you,' Molly urged.

---

28 If he'd had time, he'd have explained that it was better to be a thieving beggar than a killer and body seller. But he didn't stop to say that. Can you blame him?

'Clever thinking,' he replied and wasted a moment turning the key. The street was full of shabby people bustling about their business. The sky was as grey as the slate roofs and the cobbles slick with slime. 'But which way?' he moaned.

He headed towards the nearest street corner and saw Hare and Burke struggling up the greasy street towards him. He backed into a doorway. Too late. 'What you doing out?' little Hare cried. 'Get him, Burke.'

Boy turned and ran back past the house. The door was shaking as Mrs Burke thumped it with her mighty fist and screamed, 'Stop, thief!' Several of the shabby people heard the cries and turned to point at Boy. The keys still clattered in his fist.

'Thief!' they began to shout. 'Stop him!'

He slithered round a corner and into a road that seemed to lead past a church. A group of six men in black were carrying a coffin towards a shallow hole in the turf. The priest was a pinch-faced man in a long robe. A choirboy at his side was carrying a cross on a pole. When he heard the cries, the priest shouted, 'Stop that boy!'

The men in black dropped the coffin. The cheap wood split open and bits of tree spilled out onto the path.

The priest gasped. 'Bark!'

'Woof,' said the choirboy.

The six men in black blocked the path. No escape for Boy.

First rule of thieving: don't get caught

The men in black had linked arms. Boy tried to stop himself running into them, but his feet skidded on the cobbles and he fell on his back. His speed carried him forward like a greasy pudding off a buttery plate. He shot feet first between the legs of one man, caught the coffin-carrier's ankle and sent the man tumbling. That man fell, with arms linked to the men on either side, who fell and pulled down the ones at their sides till all six lay in a spinning, writhing, wriggling mess.

Boy picked himself up and ran on. 'Which way? Which way to Dr Wiggott's door?'

Molly answered calmly, 'Hare had never heard of Dr Wiggott. He called him Wiggle[29]. He lied to get you to help. The door you want isn't in this Waxworld.'

Boy panted. Looking over his shoulder, he saw there were still men in musty coats chasing him and hoping for some rich reward. 'So where to?'

'Back to where we started. Let's get back to the Waxworld railway and try another stop on the train,' the phone said.

'Tell me how to get back to where we started. I don't remember. It was dark. You'll have a satellite navigation built in won't you?'

Molly snorted. 'I have ... but this is 1828 and satellites haven't been invented. All I have is a map of Edinburgh from those days.'

'And do you know the name of the street where we arrived?' Boy gasped.

'No, but I'll check my memory,' she promised and went dark with a faint humming.

'Stop, thief!' the musty men cried. Boy looked over his shoulder. They were getting closer, greed in their glaring eyes. When he turned around

29 You spotted that, didn't you? I knew you would.

again, he saw his path blocked by a looming shape. 'Stop in the name of the law,' Constable Craig cried.

The constable took out his hard black stick and raised the skull-crusher over the thief's head. Boy was moving too fast to stop and the lane was too narrow for him to dodge it. Boy swung his hand back and shot it forward, so the heavy bunch of keys flew towards the crooked Constable Craig's button-busting belly.

The constable saw the iron keys jingling towards him and made to grab them. As he did he dropped the stick. Boy snatched it from the air and as he raced past he chopped it at the man's knee.

The constable cried in pain and fell in a heap. 'Assaulting a city constable … You'll hang for that.'

'Only if you catch me – first rule of thieving: don't get caught.'

Boy reached a crossroads and looked around wildly. Two men had stopped to help the lawman, but the round, red face of Burke was still there. 'Come to Will Burke, my little beauty,' the man shouted. 'I won't hurt you. I'm your friend.'

'No, I'm your friend,' Molly said suddenly. 'I've found it. Turn left . . . but hurry. . .'

I think it's time you went to sleep, laddie

The narrow streets were a black-brick, grey-stone, warped-wood maze as Boy wound his way through lefts and rights, up passages of steep steps through flocks of sheep being shepherded to market.

And in the market stalls of cloth and cotton clothing and cod, pies and pastries, carrots and crab apples, nails and nosegays, songbirds and shoes, lace and lavender, poisons and potions, barley and bread and beer and boots and blacking blocked the way. Boy threw down a churn of milk but Burke leapt over it as if it wasn't there.

Boy saw people crowding in the streets, Burke saw only money on the fleeing legs ahead. Boy was gold and all Burke had to do was reach it, clutch it, kill it.

'Down these stairs – you're doing well,' Molly said … just as a dog ran across Boy's path and tripped him. He fell and rolled but clutched the phone tight in his left hand while the hardwood constable's stick clacked on the cobbles from his right. Boy scrambled to his feet and Burke came panting and grinning his black-toothed grin at him.

'Hurr! Hurr! Time to go home. I think it's time you went to sleep, laddie[30].'

Boy looked at his captor coldly. 'I think it's time YOU went to sleep,' he said. With one smooth movement, he swept the stick up and cracked it down on the man's head. The brown hat was battered and the red face turned pale before it pitched forward into a puddle of dog piddle.

People in the market backed away from Boy and his stick. He walked calmly to the market

---

30 What a polite man. He could have said he was going to send Boy to sleep so he never woke up. That would have been cruel. Sounds much nicer if you just say it's time he went to sleep. Very thoughtful.

cross and away from the crowds.

He reached the street he thought he knew. Some of the houses with windows like empty eyes stared at him.

'This is it,' Molly said. 'Find the spot you arrived at and walk forward.'

He nodded and stood in the middle of the road. The air seemed to shimmer like the steam off a hot summer road after a shower. 'Here goes,' he said.

Boy closed his eyes and took two steps forward. He smelt the dusty air of the Waxworld where moments before there had been the stench of the streets of the city. He opened his eyes and saw a narrow railway line shine in a blue electric light.

He turned round and jumped. Burke and Hare stood there holding a barrow with a blanket-covered body. Their glass eyes stared at him.

'They're Waxworld creatures, only animated wax models. I don't think they can touch you, so long as you stay on this side of the scene,' she promised. 'You're safe.'

But he wasn't.

I collect nightsticks, you know

Boy was sure the policeman would have left the building by now. He turned a switch to reverse, pushed the pedal on the wooden locomotive and creaked backwards towards the station where he started.

'Burke and Hare were caught in the end,' Molly said as her memory whirred softly in Boy's hand. 'Hare betrayed Burke to the police. They hanged Burke and let Hare go. And Mrs Burke went free, too.'

'But Dr Knox? What about him? It was all his fault.'

'He said he bought the bodies . . . but he never knew where they came from. They let him go too. They changed the law so the surgeons could get bodies without killings.'

Boy shook his head. 'The guilty ones go free,' he sighed.

Molly laughed. 'So there's hope for you. *You're* guilty of stealing *me* . . . and *you're* still free.'

There was a creak and a screech of steel wheels on iron rails as they rolled towards the station. 'I'll get that caretaker to tell me where we'll find Wiggott's office. We can take this train to the right scene,' he said.

'I don't think so,' the phone said.

Boy squinted down the dim track and saw the bright buttons of the policeman waiting by the platform. 'Stop in the name of the law,' the man cried. 'I am PC Laurence Olivier Elloe.'

'Hello L.O. Elloe,' the boy said[31]. The caretaker stood at the door to his office with a frail and quivering old lady.

The constable pulled a notebook from his pocket and read from it. 'I have reason to believe you are in possession of stolen goods,' he said.

---

31 Remember in Chapter 2 I promised there would be no pitiful puns with L.O. Elloe's name? Well, I lied. Sorry.

Boy looked down at his left hand. 'This stick? I found it ... in an Edinburgh street.'

PC Elloe lowered his notebook. He lowered his bottom jaw. 'It's beautiful. Let me see.'

'What?' Boy laughed and handed it to the policeman.

'It's a genuine Georgian nightstick as carried by constables a hundred and ninety years ago ... look,' he cried. 'See this sign painted on the handle? That is the coat of arms of the City of Edinburgh. I collect nightsticks, you know. It's one of the reasons I joined the police force. I don't suppose you'd like to sell it, would you?'

But PC Elloe was talking to dusty air. The train was gliding away from the scene with Boy in the carriage. The thief gave a cheerful wave and PC Elloe gave a weak wave in return. 'Stop? In the name of the law?' But the name of the law can't stop a train.

Boy laughed. 'I'm free. All I have to do is find Dr Wiggott's door and collect the money. Simple.' He drove past Burke and Hare's frozen figures and on to the next scene.

'Hmmmm,' Molly hummed as the train slowed and stopped. 'Look at the scene we've stopped at and think again, Boy.'

You should be showing me thief-filled handcuffs

Igon walked back to the end of the High Street looking for another door. He found Dank Alley. Good thinking, Igon. He saw the police bicycle, pushed open the back door to the Waxworld and looked at two dithering men while Minnie Cooper slipped into the shadows to watch.

The evil assistant marched in. 'Now then, gentlemen, there is a thief in Wiggott's Wonderful Waxworld and he has stolen a phone from Arfur Loaf,' he said. 'There is a thousand pound reward for its recovery.'

'Yes and I am here to arrest him,' PC Elloe said, waving his handcuffs.

'So, Constable, may I ask why you are showing me empty handcuffs when you should be showing me thief-filled handcuffs?' Igon asked. His voice was polite but filled with steel.

Constable Elloe cleared his throat and began: 'The suspect has entered the Waxworld railway ride. . .'

'The ride goes round in a circle and ends up here, back in the station,' Mr Billy Crudge the caretaker added.

'We are waiting for the train to return. I will apprehend him and take him to the station.'

'We're already at the station,' Mr Crudge croaked.

'The police station[32].'

'Sorry.'

Igon looked at them through the gloom. 'So how do I catch the thief's train?'

'You need to take train number two, go in and follow it.' Billy Crudge pressed the foot-switch beside the line. The grimy floorboards under their feet began to tremble and in the tunnel a green light appeared.

---

32 Why do police live in stations, you ask? Ah, I answer. If they run out of police cars, they can always catch a train. Obvious really.

'Here she comes,' the policeman cried. He sprang onto the tracks and held up a hand. 'Halt in the name of the law.'

Billy Crudge took his foot off the switch. The train halted. Igon nodded. 'But the thief's train should have returned by now. Maybe he's climbed off somewhere in the ride. And people who do that disappear, I've heard. Someone needs to go after him.' The policeman looked at the caretaker with fear-filled eyes.

'Not my job,' Caretaker Crudge complained. 'My duty is here.'

'Mine too,' PC Elloe agreed and nodded till his helmet fell over his nose. 'People who go in there never come out,' he whispered.

'It is your duty,' Igon reminded him.

'Then I'll have to go,' Elloe said and jumped into the carriage. 'And I get the reward. And maybe find a clue as to the missing girl.' He pushed a pedal on the floor, cried, 'Forward in the name of the law' and rattled off into the dark.

The train trundled to a halt beside a Waxworld that showed a ship's cabin. He stepped off the train. . .

Hornswaggle the hempen halter

A head of him, the boy-thief had already stepped off train number one and onto the Waxworld scene into a ship's cabin with sea-charts and pistols scattered over it. Through the open cabin door there was a dazzling sun and a deck filled with wax sailor figures. The air changed from the cold, stale dust of the museum to the hot breeze of a tropical day with the smells of human beings and gunpowder and dirt and sea air.

'Where am I?' he muttered into the phone. The fake starry sky of Wiggott's Waxworld had vanished and a copper sun was glowing in a dry and cloudless sky.

'Read the label,' Molly's voice said from the phone[33].

A wax figure of a man in a red jacket with golden buttons stood beside a printed board.

It read:

Captain Edward 'Blackbeard' Teach – Pirate
Aboard *Queen Anne's Revenge*
November 1718

(Remember: Danger – Do not leave the train)

The wax man had eyes as mad as a box of frogs and a round red face. A familiar face topped by black bear hair. Most of that face was hidden

---

33 'Read the label'. Good advice. If you have a bottle and the label says *Poison*, then don't drink it. Reading the label on a poison bottle can save your life. Give it to a passing traffic warden.

behind a thick black beard that curled like a hundred little helter-skelters.

Beside him was a skinny man with a ferret face. Boy stared hard at them. The clothes were different – the beard was added – but they were the faces of two evil men he'd met before.

'Burke and Hare?' he breathed.

Suddenly, the beard on the waxwork began to blow in the breeze and the little ferret-man twitched and began to hop from foot to foot.

'Naval cutter off the starboard bow, Captain,' he said in a whining voice, half excited, half afraid.

The man with the beard, Captain Teach, raised a spyglass to his eye, looked at the sailing ship ploughing through the waves towards them and roared till his red face turned purple. 'Avast, me hearties! It be the scurvy bilge-rats of the navy, so let's belay those hornpipes, stow yer deadlights, hornswaggle the hempen halter, grab your grapeshot, scrape the barnacles off me rudder and shiver me timbers, me hearties, me picaroons, me scallywag rapscalliony buckos. And remember. . .' He paused for breath – well, quite a few breaths – and went on with a twist to his fat lips, 'Fried eggs tell no lies.'

Boy looked around the deck of the ship as it rose and fell in the rippling sea. A gang of ragged seamen were climbing ropes, hauling on sails, polishing cannons on the decks and stacking cannonballs into pyramids. They froze, and frowns fell across their filthy faces.

The little man who looked a lot like Hare sighed. 'Captain Teach.'

'Yes, Mister Mate Israel Hands?'

'The crew are foreign. Spanish, French, Dutch.'

'I knows that, Israel Hands.'

'So they don't understand you when you talk piratical. Speak English, speak it slow and stop talking like a common man from the slums of Bristol.'

Captain Teach began to fasten two belts across his shoulders. Each held three pistols. He sniffed and muttered, 'I like talking piratical. I mean to say... I'm a pirate.'

'Yes, sir, but the men don't understand.'

The mate turned to face the crew. 'Navy,'

he said pointing. Then he did a mime of being choked by a rope. 'Fight or they hang you.'

The men began to run to haul up sails and load the cannon.

Boy just smiled and said softly, 'Pirates. A ship full of treasure. Wonderful.'

And from his pocket Molly's voice jangled, 'Idiot.'

The captain turned his fierce face to Boy. 'Who are you calling an idiot?' he roared. 'Israel Hands, fire this cabin-boy from a cannon.'

You can use me as a human shield

Boy groaned and hissed at the phone in his pocket. 'Now look what you've done.'

The black-bearded captain grabbed him by the front of his shirt and pulled his face so close to the matted beard that Boy could smell the hair. It smelled of smoke.

'I am going to shoot you straight at that naval ship. That'll teach you to call the great Captain Teach an idiot.'

'No it won't,' Boy snapped, wriggling away from the choking smoke.

'Won't what?'

'Won't teach me a lesson. I'll be too dead to learn the lesson. It would be far better if you gave me a cutlass and sent me to fight the navy when they board your ship,' Boy said. 'You can use me as a human shield.'

'A what?' the black-bearded man said.

'Great idea,' Israel Hands said. 'Stand the lad in front of you and use him as a shield. If they shoot him, you'll have your revenge *and* he'll save your life, Captain.'

'A really great idea,' the captain said. 'I'm glad I thought of it.'

'But hurry,' Israel Hands said. 'They're catching us. I reckon they'll be alongside in twenty or thirty minutes.'

The captain nodded. 'Just enough time to barber my beard. Send for the barber.'

'Sorry captain, you marooned him on an island off New Providence last week. You said he messed up your curls.'

'Terrible man,' Captain Teach sighed. 'And an even worse barber. This cabin-boy can do it for me before I use him as a human shield.'

Boy shrugged, 'What do you want me to do?'

117

Teach's eyes went as narrow as a frog's mouth. 'You should know what to do – everybody knows about the famous Blackbeard. Unless you're a navy spy ... in which case, I'll have you fired from the mouth of a cannon.'

'He wouldn't fit,' Molly the phone muttered.

'Go and get the curling irons from my cabin,' Teach ordered.

Boy ran onto the deck, pulled out the phone and hissed, 'Where's the cabin? I'm supposed to know these things ... and what do I do with his beard?'

The phone hummed softly and clicked and beeped and bipped and cleaked. 'I've found it,' Molly said. 'Ah ... you're in luck ... so long as the navy doesn't kill you first.'

Boy looked over the blue-green sea towards the navy ship and saw a pale face staring at him from the deck of the enemy. It was a face he'd seen before. He waved.

That seemed to set the navy officers off running. A minute later there was a puff of smoke and Boy saw a cannonball soar into the air then swoop down towards his head. He waited to be crushed like an egg[34].

---

34 'Who can it be?' you gasp. 'Wait and see,' I reply.

A policeman's gotta do
what a policeman's gotta do

You may have guessed the familiar face on the navy ship belonged PC Elloe. 'How did he arrive there?' you ask. I shall tell you because I am so very kind to you.

The policemen had ridden on the little electric train car. He was trembling like a tree in a gale ... like a scarecrow when you show it a box of matches ... like a sausage when you show it a frying pan.

The Waxworld had the gloom of a doom-filled tomb. Bulbs like glow-worms sparkled in the high ceiling, but they only gave a faint light.

The electric train whirred and clanked over the rusting rails. It ran slowly on a twisting trail through the tomb-gloom-room. But he didn't follow the track that Boy had travelled down. Mr Crudge the caretaker pushed buttons on a control panel in his office. The train switched and twitched around lopping lines. It was almost as if the caretaker had wanted the boy-thief to escape and deliver the phone to Dr Wiggott. So, at each turn there was a new scene for the police-person passenger to view. (Did I mention he was trembling?)

Dust-covered wax figures stood in painted wooden scenes from the past. He rattled past ancient Rome then found himself rolling past plains in the Wild West of America, then in a dungeon from the Middle Ages, then face-to-face with a villainous Victorian.

It was a world tour of every age and a dozen countries. They had just one thing the same: the figures were wax models of the most evil people who ever lived. The matted hair and rotting clothes on the sawdust-stuffed bodies, the shabby scenes and the paint-peeling walls all looked harmless enough. We could have told him, 'Don't look at the eyes, PC Elloe. Don't look at the eyes or you'll start trembling. Oh, sorry, you already are.'

The glass eyes in the wicked wax faces glittered in the green light on the front of the electric train. The eyes seemed to follow the petrified PC on his train trip. They watched him come and they watched him go. It was almost as if they wished they could get their wax hands around his... Enough[35]!

Another green-lit electric train stood on the track ahead. It was empty.

There was a crackle and a hiss. PC Elloe thought the train was making the noise. But it was the ancient speakers in the run-down Waxworld sparking into life. 'Visitors please stay on the train. It is forbidden to step off the train at any time. This could be very dangerous.'

The policeman shook and called up to the speaker. 'I don't want to get off the train ... but a policeman's gotta do what a policeman's gotta do.'

PC Elloe looked at the label on the Waxworld:

35 I don't know if this is frightening you, but it's scaring the sweat out of me.

Captain Edward 'Blackbeard' Teach – Pirate
Aboard *Queen Anne's Revenge*
November 1718

(Remember: Danger – Do not leave the train)

He left the train. 'A policeman's gotta do what a policeman's gotta do,' he mumbled to himself. 'Even if it means risking his life to capture a bad-boy burglar.'

How very dare he?

Elloe stepped forward. Elloe stumbled through the cabin door onto the ship's deck. The floor seemed to move under his feet and a spray of salty water sprinkled his pale face. He rubbed it from his stinging eyes then looked around.

Men stood around. They were dressed, like him, in dark blue uniforms with silver buttons. A man in a high, white collar stood on a barrel beside the mast and waved a pistol. He shouted over the noise of the rushing, splashing sea. 'At the ready, brave lads. That's Blackbeard's ship ahead,' he said.

PC Elloe looked at where the officer was pointing. A ship with tattered sails and a black flag was wallowing through the waves ahead of them.

'And what do we do when we catch *Queen Anne's Revenge*?' a sailor called.

'Aye, Captain Maynard. What do we do?' the crew repeated.

'We board her and tell the crew to surrender. If they refuse, we shoot them. Spare the crew if you can. Just make sure the man with the black beard is captured or killed.'

'Killed? We can't do that!' PC Elloe squeaked. 'He has to have a fair trial.'

The sailors laughed. 'Blackbeard won't go around giving fair trials before he tries to blow us out of the water.'

'I'm only here to arrest a boy – a thief. I have to take him back in handcuffs.'

Maynard glared at Elloe. 'Tell you what, officer, we'll fire a shot across the bows of *Queen Anne's Revenge*. That's a warning. It gives him a chance to surrender.'

'Ooooh,' PC Elloe groaned. 'I hope you don't hurt anybody.'

Maynard grinned. '*I* won't hurt *anyone* ... because *you're* going to fire the cannon. Take the six-pounder in the bows.'

'Ooooh,' Elloe gasped and walked on wobbling legs towards the cannon.

He looked across the rolling waves. The thief looked back. Boy's captor was just a wave away.

So Boy waved.

It was a mistake. It made PC Elloe angry. It made him miss his aim. 'How dare he mock the uniform of Wildpool Police?' he gasped. 'How very dare he?'

He touched the fuse to the end of the cannon. It hissed and spat and went silent for half a moment. What he forgot to do was aim it in front of the pirate ship, the way captain Maynard had ordered[36].

The cannonball shot towards the deck of Blackbeard's ship.

36 A tip for you when you next fire a cannon at an enemy ship. Do it when you are calm. Don't do it in a raging rush or something terrible may happen ... or you could burn your finger on the fuse.

They'll pay for that...

In fact, that cannonball was heading for Boy's head.

The thief's mouth fell open, empty as a pauper's purse. He stared. He waited to die. The cabin door crashed open and a large woman stepped on deck. Her red jacket was rolled up to the elbows and her blue trousers were cut off at the knees. She had a fierce face with two chins and greasy hair tied back like Mrs Burke. Actually, she looked exactly like Mrs Burke – or Lady Greystone.

The woman glanced up at the black ball in the

sky that was growing larger with every instant of time. 'Duck!' she shouted at Boy.

He stayed frozen. The cannonball was as large as his head and an arm's length away when she gave him a lazy push. Boy fell to the deck a moment before the ball struck the boards, bounced with the sound of a splintered tree and disappeared over the other side into the ocean.

'Well done, Mrs Teach,' Israel Hands chuckled.

The woman's red-blotched face glared at the navy ship. 'They're supposed to fire a warning shot first. Supposed to give us a chance to surrender.'

'Maybe the gunner was just a rotten shot,' Israel Hands shrugged.

Boy sat up and looked at the man behind the enemy ship. 'I think he is,' he said.

Blackbeard roared, 'They'll pay for that ... after I've had me beard fixed. We have ten minutes before they're alongside. Get up, boy, and get me beard in fighting trim,' the captain commanded.

Boy spread his hands, helpless. 'How?'

'I'll show you,' Mrs Teach offered. She pulled

a knife from her belt, went to a cannon and chopped a length of the thin rope they used as a fuse. With fingers that flew like flustered finches, frightened falcons or fussing flycatchers, she sliced the fuse into pieces as long as Boy's fingers. Mrs Teach began to curl her husband's beard with iron tongs heated in the cooking stove, then tied the pieces of fuse into the captain's beard. Boy copied.

Molly's phone flashed a message:

> Blackbeard had the fuses tied into his beard *and* stuck under his hat. He lit them so they burned slowly. His whole head was surrounded by smoke and it scared the pants off the people he robbed. They thought he was a devil.

'Thanks,' Boy muttered and carried on with his work.

'Five minutes till they're alongside,' Israel Hands cried. He ran to the side of a cannon where a slow fuse was already burning, ready to light the gunpowder, and brought it to his captain. Boy and Mrs Teach used that fuse to light the fuses in Teach's beard and soon his face was hidden behind a smoking curtain like a damp bonfire.

The crew fell silent and waited for the battle ahead. The only sounds were the wind cracking in the sails, the ropes slapping on the decks and the planks creaking as the ship rocked. Boy muttered, 'As soon as they start fighting, I'll go below, steal his treasure and escape from that policemen.'

'I told you before, you're an idiot,' Molly answered. 'Blackbeard's treasure isn't what you think[37].'

---

37 You knew that. You probably learned it at school. But Boy never went to school ... at least he went to a school for thieves, and that doesn't count.

Ugly mug ... a bit like yours

Meanwhile, at the platform in Wiggott's Wonderful Waxworld, the shambling, limping man in black stopped shambling and limping. He strode along the platform. The walls of warped wood and soot-stained stone looked down.

He peered at Caretaker Crudge. 'You know where Boy is headed. Tell me and I'll lie in wait for him.'

'There's a secret plan in my office. It shows the way behind the scenes to Dr Wiggott's secret office. But it's so secret I'm not even allowed to tell anyone about it. Dr Wiggott is a private person. He doesn't like to be disturbed. It's more than me job's worth.'

Igon tried Crudge's door. It was locked. Loaf's evil servant sighed and reached into his pocket. He pulled out a matchbox. 'In this box I have a box of termites. Termites eat wood. These are super-termites, bred in Loaf Tower. They will eat your door in ten minutes. What will you do without a door?'

'Get a draft,' Crudge replied. 'Probably catch me death of cold.'

'So open it in the name of the Loaf,' Igon demanded.

The caretaker unlocked the creaking door. More paint fell off. Any termite army would have a crumbly meal[38].

Igon lifted his eyepatch so he could see into the gloomy room.

'So what's the eyepatch for?' Billy Crudge asked.

Igon shrugged. 'Just to make me look evil,' he said. 'Scares the enemies of Arfur Loaf.'

---

38 Some people like crumble. They like apple crumble. My favourite is blackberry crumble. Of course, it's not so tasty as an old wooden door ... if you're a termite.

'A bit like the Vikings with their big bully beards,' the caretaker nodded and looked towards the Waxworld railway. 'The peasants were scared just looking at them.'

The salty scent of the sea drifted from the maze of worlds. The old man knew someone had opened a path into a sea-world somewhere.

'Vikings?' Igon asked. 'Is that where Wiggott is hiding? I may as well take train number three and look for the Viking Waxworld. No point fumbling my way through the passageways.'

'The peasants usually gave up without a fight,' Billy Crudge was going on, 'when they saw a Viking's hideous visage.'

'Hideous visage?' Igon asked.

'Ugly mug ... a bit like yours,' Crudge explained.

'Thanks.'

'Don't mention it.'

Train number three rolled up to the platform and Igon climbed aboard. An old lady slipped in to hide in the shadows and watch. It was Minnie Cooper. Snooper.

Show him how ruthless you are

But Boy wasn't in a Viking world ... yet. He was on board Blackbeard's ship, *Queen Anne's Revenge*.

As the navy ship pulled alongside, Blackbeard grabbed Boy and held him just below his smoking beard. He called out to the navy vessel, 'Avast and belay, Captain Maynard. By me deadlights, ye can hornswaggle yer hempen halter, or I'll buckshot the boyo.'

Maynard scratched his head. 'What does that mean, Teach?'

Mrs Teach sighed. 'It means go away or he'll

shoot the boy.'

Israel Hands put in, 'And fried eggs tell no lies – neither does Captain Teach.'

'Give yourself up, you thief!' Maynard called.

PC Laurence Olivier Elloe stepped onto the side rail of the navy ship and shouted, 'Yes, give yourself up, you theeeeee—ooops!' The two ships had bumped.

PC Elloe fell forward onto his face. He landed on the deck of *Queen Anne's Revenge* with a clatter of handcuffs, radio, notebook (with pencil), baton and silver buttons ... and a squidge of cheese sandwiches (with pickle) that his mother had packed for him that morning.

The ships drifted apart. The sailors on the naval ship dropped anchor and waited an arm's length away to see what would happen next.

Elloe rolled onto his back and found himself looking into the surprised faces of a pirate crew. The policeman picked himself up, brushed himself down and pulled out his baton. 'I arrest you and warn you I'll write down anything you say.'

'What's the charge?' Blackbeard leered. His words jeered. His beard sneered (or so it appeared).

Elloe blinked. 'Well, I could charge you with smoking in a public place, sir. But, as it happens, I wasn't talking to you, sir, I was talking to the boy. I am arresting him for the theft of a phone.'

'A bone?' Mrs Teach raged. 'My husband, Edward Teach, is the most famous man in the world. He is the greatest pirate ever to walk the Seven Seas. When he dies the pirate world will cry enough tears to make it eight seas. When you've shot him down and hanged him, that is.'

'Steady on, Mabel,' Blackbeard muttered.

'Show him how ruthless you are, Edward!' his wife screamed. 'Shoot the boy in cold blood. And when your pistol is empty, draw your cutlass and fight every sailor on the naval ship, five at a time ... no, ten at a time, till they cut you to pieces and leave you weltering in your gore on the deck.'

'Weltering? What does that mean, Mabel?'

'Dunno, Edward. I saw it in a play once. The hero said he'd leave the villain weltering in his own gore. He had a lovely moustache.'

'But I can't shoot the boy,' Blackbeard moaned.

'A brave and terrible man like you can blow out his brains. Leave them weltering on the sweltering deck.'

'I would if I could, but I am not able, Mabel,' he said. 'He's gone.' And so he had. Boy was no longer there. He was gone with the wind. Vanished into thin hair[39].

---

39 When I say 'thin hair' I mean it was thinner than the hair on Captain Teach's black beard but not so thin as the hair on an egg.

Where would he keep his treasure?

Boy had slipped away under the cover of the choking, smoking beard. He had run down a short flight of stairs that led to a door. He opened it and found himself in the lantern-lit gloom below the deck.

'Where would he keep his treasure?' he muttered.

Molly's voice on the phone seemed to growl, 'I have been trying to tell you. Pirates didn't steal treasure. They stole stuff they could sell.'

Boy lifted the lantern off its hook and looked into the shadows. The hold of the ship was full of sacks and wooden boxes. Boy laughed. 'They robbed Spanish galleons full of gold and silver. I heard about them when I was very young in the orphanage.'

'I didn't know you were an orphan,' Molly said softly.

'I'm not now. I'm an apprentice thief. And I'm here to steal Blackbeard's gold.'

'No,' Molly said. 'You're here to sell me to Dr Wiggott.'

'That's true,' Boy nodded. 'But a pocket full of Spanish gold would be useful.'

The phone bleeped, Molly's face faded and the screen showed a page from a book. A mechanical voice began to read:

Blackbeard stole from merchant ships. In one raid he took one hundred and twenty barrels of flour and another hundred barrels of wine. His crew stole sugar and maps and were very fond of stealing fine clothes. When they attacked a slave ship they made some of the slaves into sailors and set the others free.

'No gold?' Boy groaned.

'The days of the Spanish treasure ships were a hundred and fifty years before Blackbeard was even born.'

Boy kicked a sack and a cloud of white flour dusted the air while spiders scuttled for the dark cracks in the boards. 'Flour,' he snorted. 'I guess I'll have to go on with my search for Dr Wiggott and that reward.'

'What if I don't *want* to be handed over to Dr Wiggott?' Molly complained.

Boy shook his head. 'You're a phone. You can't decide who owns you.'

'Am I? Am I just a phone?' she whispered.

'Plastic case with a screen and buttons. You're a phone. Dr Wiggott is behind one of the Waxworld scenes. Once I find him I'll hand you over. End of story.'

'You don't know *which* scene Wiggott's office is behind, do you? And every one holds a dangerous story. Anyone could come alive and get you killed.'

Boy laughed. 'Wildpool is dangerous. I'm not dead yet.'

'You *know* Wildpool. It's your home. This is the North Atlantic three hundred years ago.'

'I'm an expert thief. I'll escape. I always do.'

'No you won't,' she hissed. 'You got greedy and careless. You broke rule number two of the Burglar Code.'

Boy swallowed hard. 'So I did[40].'

---

40 You would only be interested in burglar rule number two if you were planning to become a burglar. If you *are* interested, then I hope you feel ashamed of yourself.

I should charge you with lying to a policeman

'*Only break* in *to a place if you're sure there's another way* out,' Molly said.

'I know that – I mean I *forgot* it, but I *knew* it. How did *you* know?'

'I found it on the internet. I seem to know most things except...'

'Except?'

'Except how my mind – Molly's mind – is trapped inside this phone,' Molly murmured. 'But your problem is bigger than mine at the moment.'

The hold with the cargo was below the deck

and now the deck above their heads was pounding with pirate and naval boots. 'Wait!' came a cry. The drumming feet went still and the voice of PC L.O. Elloe drifted down. 'Find the boy-thief.'

Mrs Teach cackled. 'He's a clever one, that lad. We could use him in the crew.'

'He's so clever we could make him captain,' Israel Hands added.

'Steady on, Israel,' Blackbeard wailed. 'That's mutiny, that is.'

'Only joking, Captain Teach,' Israel Hands laughed.

'Just don't tell this law officer where the lad is,' Mrs Teach said sternly.

'I don't *know* where he is,' Blackbeard said. 'The only place he could be is down the stairs in the ship's hold with our loot.'

'Yes,' Mrs Teach groaned. 'Just don't tell this weedy lawman that.'

'Sorry, dear, I won't,' Blackbeard promised.

'Aha, so he's in the hold, is he?' PC Elloe cried.

'No,' the pirate crew cried and lied with one voice[41].

---

41 Don't be shocked. Pirates lie. It's their job. Only fried eggs tell no lies.

'Where are the stairs?' Elloe asked.

'They're not behind you,' the pirates told him.

'Aha! There they are ... behind me. You lied. I should charge you with lying to a policeman. There's a reward for his capture.'

'Let's help the officer, lads,' Israel Hands roared.

'What's a policeman?' Blackbeard asked.

Boy and Molly heard the PC's boots clumping down the wooden steps.

'Burglar rule number nine,' the phone said.

'*Use whatever is handy*,' Boy nodded. He jumped across the hold, grabbed a wine barrel and rolled it to the door. The door was just beginning to open when the barrel hit it and slammed it shut.

'Ooooh, me nose,' came the cry of the pitiful policeman.

I'm very attached to me head

'So now you've turned your treasure cave into a prison,' Molly said.

But Boy ignored her and was using the lantern to look quickly around the ship's hold. 'Those barrels couldn't get through that door,' he said. 'The pirates must have lowered them in through a hatch in the deck.'

'Well done,' Molly said. 'That's your way out, then.'

Boy stood on a barrel and pushed up on the ceiling of his prison. The hatch cover slid along. He looked out. There was a crew of pirates between him and the cabin door that he'd entered from – his way back to Wiggott's Wonderful Waxworld wailway... I mean *railway*.

PC Elloe was hitting the door to the treasure store with his truncheon and it was starting to crack. 'You can pay for that,' Blackbeard roared. Boy knew that if he stayed there another five minutes, the pirates would swarm in and capture him. If he climbed out, the pirates would capture him.

He heaved up the lid of a wooden chest with leather hinges. Inside were some rich clothes of velvet and silk. He plunged his hands in and pulled out a pair of blue lady's knickers with long legs to them. He tied a knot in each leg then tore the cord that fastened the top of a bag of flour. He used his hands to stuff the silk pants full of flour.

The door was cracking and splinters spilled onto the floor of the hold as he threw the flour-filled knickers over his shoulder. 'You may be good at finding *facts*,' he said to Molly. 'But I'm better at *thinking*.'

He pushed the hatch further open and climbed

through the gap. Before any of the people on deck saw him, he was halfway up the rope-rigging on the mast. Mrs Teach was the first to see him. 'Edward ... he's here,' she cried.

The pirates and the naval sailors ran to the foot of the mast. PC Elloe came up the steps, back onto the deck, and pushed his way to the front. 'Give yourself up, boy. You are at the wrong end of a one-way street. The only way is down. You are trapped.'

Boy grinned, 'No, Constable Clown. *You* are trapped.' He swung the flour-filled knickers off his shoulder and held it over the heads of the people below.

Mrs Teach screamed, 'Them's me best blue buttoned bloomers, Edward! The ones we nicked from that French ship. Lovely silk bloomers. Give them back, boy,' the captain's wife raged.

'I've nicked your knickers. They're full of gunpowder. I will drop them on your husband's head and they'll burst. The lighted fuses in his beard will explode and blow his head off.'

'Steady on,' Blackbeard grumbled. 'I'm very attached to me head.'

'And I'm very attached to my best blue buttoned bloomers,' his wife said, and she looked as grim as grandma with gout. 'I'm going up to get them back,' she said and started to climb.

Boy raised the pants and shrugged. 'I warned you. . .[42]'

---

42 He did. That was very sporting of him. He could have just dropped the pants and covered their fine (stolen) piratical clothes in flour. The boy had flour-power in his hands.

I said he's up to no good

Meanwhile, just inside the back door to Wiggott's Wonderful Waxworld, one of the Ladies Who Crunch stepped out of the shadows. It was, of course, Minnie Cooper.

She'd watched Arfur Loaf's assistant, Igon, hobble across to the Waxworld train and set off into the dusky dark displays.

'He's up to no good,' Minnie said.

Mister Crudge jumped a little. 'I'd forgotten you were there, Minnie.'

'I'm silent as a cat, sly as a fox and I have the ears of a bat,' she boasted.

Billy Crudge nodded. 'Edna always said you were batty.'

'Did she?'

'Yes. She says if brains were raisins you'd be a plain teacake. Now, what were you saying?'

'I said he's up to no good, that Igon character.'

'He looks shifty,' the caretaker agreed.

'You can see it in his eyes,' Minnie Cooper said, her bottom lip trembling like a jelly[43].

'But he's only got one eye,' Mr Crudge pointed out. 'How can you see it in his eyes when he only has one eye you can see?'

Minnie clamped her trembling lips tight shut and tried to keep her temper. 'I can see it in the way his ONE eye keeps looking around. He doesn't want to be followed. He is up to no good,' she repeated.

'It's none of our business,' the old man sniffed.

Minnie glared through her glasses at the man in the frayed and faded grey coat. 'What about if we're right? Me and Edna and Marjorie Doors all agree. What about if he knows something about the missing girl? What if he gets his hands on

43 That reminds me of a joke. Question: 'What trembles on the bottom of the ocean? Answer: A nervous wreck. (Don't blame me, mate. I never said it was a GOOD joke.)

that phone? Eh, Billy Crudge? Eh? Answer me that.'

'What can we do about it?' Mr Crudge shrugged.

'I plan to follow him. See where he goes. Unmask him.'

'Pull his eyepatch off, you mean?'

Minnie looked to the fake starry skies. 'No I do NOT mean rip his eyepatch off. I plan to follow him. See where he goes and report back to Edna. If we find where he's holding the girl prisoner, then we'll call the police and claim the reward.'

'Reward?'

'A thousand pounds,' Minnie said pointing at the advert printed in the paper she pulled from her pocket. 'What are you waiting for?'

'I'm still waiting for you to pay me a pound to enter the Waxworld,' Mr Crudge said.

'I am here because your Edna sent me,' Minnie said and pushed her spectacles up her nose so she could burn the caretaker with her fierce glare. 'Edna would not be happy if I told her you charged a poor, penniless pensioner to enter your pathetic, plastic palace, would she?'

'No,' Billy Crudge sighed miserably.

'What would she do with that lovely, fresh steak pie she bought for your dinner?'

'Feed it to the dog.'

'So are you going to charge me?'

'A pound.'

'What? Aren't you afraid of seeing your dinner in the dog?' she gasped.

'We haven't got a dog,' the man grinned. 'And the goldfish doesn't like steak pie.'

Taking risks
is my job

Captain Teach grabbed his wife and stopped her climbing up to Boy on the mast. 'Too dangerous, my little swamp duck. Leave it to the law officer.'

PC Elloe found all the crew looking at him. He gave a small cough then looked up at Boy. 'This is a hostage situation,' he explained to the sailors. 'Sadly, I don't do my hostage training till next month.'

'Leave it to me,' Mrs Teach sighed. She looked at the men on the deck. There will be a golden doubloon to the first man to climb the mast and get my best blue buttoned bloomers back or die in the effort.'

No one moved. No one wanted to be blown apart for blue bloomers. PC Elloe faced the men. 'Never forget that wonderful poem by Mrs Hemans.'

'Never heard of it,' Israel Hands said with a shrug.

'We all learned it at school,' the policeman said with a happy chuckle. Then he recited it:

The boy stood on the burning deck,
Whence all but he had fled;
The flame that lit the battle's wreck,
Shone round him o'er the dead.

Mrs Teach shook the PC and snapped, 'The deck isn't burning, and there aren't any dead.'

PC Elloe turned pink. 'No ... no ... not *yet*. But there will be when he drops that gunpowder. The point is, we need a hero like the boy that stood on the burning deck.'

'So why don't *you* go up there?' Blackbeard asked.

'I would. I'd be up there like a squirrel up a skyscraper. But I'm scared of heights.'

The phone buzzed and Boy looked at it. There was a poem on the screen that Molly had found. The sailors looked on amazed as Boy laughed and read it aloud...

> *The boy stood on the burning deck.*
> *His lips were all a-quiver.*
> *He gave a cough, his leg fell off*
> *And floated down the river.*

The policeman's pink face turned an angry red. 'You should not be making fun of such a great poem. I have given you your last warning.'

'Oh, I know,' Boy jeered. 'But I'm still here. What are you going to do about it?'

'I will get Captain Teach to shoot you with his pistol. That'll teach you... I mean *teach* you, not Captain Teach you.'

The young thief held out the silk knickers. 'And when I fall, the gunpowder will fall and set fire to the ship and we'll all be on a burning deck. Go on. Shoot.'

Molly gasped. 'You're taking a risk, Boy,' she said.

'Taking risks is my job,' he told her. 'I don't need you to argue with me. I need you to find me a way across that crowded deck to the cabin door and back to Wiggott's.'

The phone hummed[44] ... and an old black-and-white movie shimmered on the screen.

'Wait,' Boy cried, and everyone went quiet as Boy watched scenes from the movie *Captain Blood*.

---

44 It's not only phones that hum. Lots of people hum, too. Usually because they don't know the words.

What would Captain Blood do?

The film flickered to a halt. Molly's face appeared on the screen again. 'See what you have to do?'

Boy nodded. 'You're the cleverest phone I've ever met,' he said. He put the phone safely in his pocket and turned to the crew. 'I am Captain Blood,' he said.

'You never said,' Mrs Teach shouted. 'What do you want with my best blue buttoned bloomers, Captain Blood?'

'I am the greatest pirate ever to sail the seas,' Boy went on.

'No,' Blackbeard objected, '*I'm* the greatest pirate ever to sail the seas.'

Boy nodded. 'You are, sir. I meant to say, I am the *second*-greatest pirate ever to sail the seas. I am on your side. We are all thieves together.'

The pirates muttered and agreed. Molly whispered a line from the *Captain Blood* movie and Boy repeated it aloud. 'It's the world against us and us against the world.'

The pirates cheered. 'Well said, lad,' Israel Hands called.

'I wish I'd said that,' Blackbeard groaned.

Boy repeated the movie script almost word for word.

We are outlaws in our own land and homeless outcasts in any other. We are desperate men; we go to seek a desperate fortune. We are a brotherhood of buccaneers. We practise the trade of piracy on the high seas. We, the hunted, will now hunt.

'Hunt who?' Blackbeard asked. He turned to his wife and sighed, 'I was just saying, wish I could make fine speeches like that.'

Boy read the next speech.

Up that rigging, you monkeys[45]. Aloft. There's no chains to hold you now. Break out those sails and watch them fill with the wind that's carrying us all to freedom.

Israel Hands turned to the pirates. 'He means let's sail away from the navy ship to freedom.'

The crew scuttled across the deck to haul on ropes to raise the sails, load the cannon and raise the anchor. Two of them danced a hornpipe. The sailors on the navy ship looked across, amazed. The most ruthless pirates looked back at them and stuck out their tongues.

All the while, Blackbeard roared them on. 'Belay those deadlights, stow yer hornpipes, hornswaggle the barnacles, grab your hempen halter, scrape the grapeshot off me timbers and shiver me rudder, me hearties, me picaroons, me

45 Calling those putrid pirates 'monkeys' was a huge insult ... to monkeys.

scallywag rapscalliony buckos. Ooooh... I wish I knew what all that meant.'

Molly called, 'Now's the time to run across the deck and get to the gateway door back to Wiggott's.'

But PC Elloe stood firm as pirates swirled around him. 'I can't get past the policeman,' Boy moaned. 'What would Captain Blood do?'

Molly showed him the movie...

Me best blue
buttoned bloomers

'Of course,' Boy laughed. He watched Captain Blood grab a rope and swing across from mast to mast till he was safely away from his hunters. The young thief grabbed a rope. He swung over PC Elloe's head. He forgot he was carrying the flour-filled knickers.

They fell. At the feet of PC Elloe.

Mrs Teach screamed, 'Me best blue buttoned bloomers!'

Captain Teach cried, 'Me head's gonna be blown off!'

The pirates had stopped hauling, hornpiping,

hornswaggling and hempen haltering when the bloomers hit the deck. They split open – the bloomers, not the pirates. A cloud of flour flew and made a massive mound on the deck[46].

Boy dropped to the deck. At that moment a light breeze made the two ships bump. PC Elloe held tight to the mast, but boy stumbled and fell. PC Elloe raised his truncheon and took a step towards the helpless boy-thief as he landed between the two cabin doors.

But as the ships collided they squeezed the water between them and sent a wave of spray onto the deck and over the heap of flour. The dry flour turned into damp and very sticky dough. The policeman's left foot was stuck fast and it made him wobble on his weedy legs. He threw his right leg forward to steady himself and planted it into the dough. He was stuck fast.

'That wave's wetted the gunpowder and saved us all!' Israel Hands cried.

'It's also wetted my best blue buttoned bloomers!' Mrs Teach sobbed. 'They'll be ruined.'

'Help me!' Elloe wailed. He grabbed for the

---

46 Mrs Teach was a large lady, so her bloomers were a little larger than a pirate ship's sail. They held a lot of flour.

knees of his trousers and tried to pull his feet free. That made him drop his truncheon.

Boy rose to his feet and came closer to the officer till he stood at the edge of the piratical paste. 'Sorry, Constable. I'd love to help, but no one has the money to pay me to set you free.'

'Pay you?' Elloe groaned as he struggled.

'Yes,' Boy grinned. 'It would cost you a lot of dough. Geddit?'

From his pocket there came a soft moan. 'That was a very bad joke, Boy.'

His smile became as wide as a lifeboat. 'I have to dash. I can't *loaf* around here all day. Geddit?'

'I get it,' Blackbeard nodded. 'Very funny.'

'No it's not,' Elloe cried. 'It's a matter of life or death.'

'What was that?' Israel Hands said, joining in the fun. 'A matter of *loaf* or death?'

Elloe turned purple in the face with anger and with the struggle under the hot sun that baked the dough harder. He pointed at Boy and said, 'When I get you, you're toast.'

At that the whole crew roared with laughter.

Boy walked over to the pair of cabin doors. 'Make sure you choose the right door,' Molly warned.

But Boy was having too much fun to listen to her warning. He turned back and waved goodbye to PC Elloe. 'Sorry to leave you in a jam.'

He ran towards the right door. The door on the right. But was it the right door?

He opened the door, stepped through without looking . . . and tumbled forward into deep, dark, cold water. Before his head went under he heard Molly moan, 'Idiot.'

Only you can rescue me

The cold water was such a shock that Boy gasped when it hit him. Gasping is not a good idea when you are underwater. Don't try it. This water was shallow and the sand beneath his feet firm.

As his head broke through the surface he found there was no pirate ship in sight. There was a blood-red sunrise over the water and the nearest land seemed to be a small island with a tall building on the top of a hill. He waded steadily towards it, a chill wind blowing through his hair.

The tide seemed to be going out because the path he was on rose above the waves.

'Land or island?' Boy asked as he shivered inside his clothes.

'Just as well I'm waterproof,' the phone told him[47].

'You deserved to drown,' he said. 'You sent me through the wrong door.'

'I told you to take the right door – the one on the left. The one you took into Blackbeard's world.'

'You should have told me to take the one on the left – not the right door.'

'You were too busy making jokes to pay attention,' Molly argued.

'You're so smart but you're just a smartphone. You don't understand what it's like being human.'

'I do,' she said with panic in her voice. 'I think I am human.'

Boy snorted. 'Arfur Loaf is clever, but he can't squeeze a girl into a phone. Sorry. Even he can't do that.'

He set off walking towards the island, where

---

47 'Aha,' you cry, 'I am waterproof too … otherwise my blood would leak out.' What she meant was her phone case was waterproof. Most are not – which is why you should not have a bath while you text a friend.

there were signs of human life. Smoke rose from some of the thatched wooden buildings that surrounded the large one on the hill.

'Listen, Boy, I keep getting flashes through the mists of my memory. Memories of when I was a girl – a human like you.'

'Impossible. Arfur Loaf can't. . .'

'No. Listen. I'm not inside this phone. Only my mind is – I remember now. My name is Molly Maltby. I was kidnapped. I've been wired up to a transmitter. You're holding a computer powered by brain power. *My* brain's power.'

Boy stopped. He shivered again in the morning breeze. 'So where's your body?' he asked.

'I think it's in Arfur Loaf's tower. You have to rescue me, Boy. I mean rescue the *real* me – not just my mind. My kidnapped body. Mum and Dad must be sick with worry by now. Only you know I'm there. Only you can rescue me.'

'Only you can get me out of this weird Waxworld,' he replied.

'We need one another,' Molly Maltby said. 'I help you so you can help me. No more arguing?'

'I can't promise that,' Boy muttered as he

jogged along the path to the island to try and unfreeze his blood. 'Mum and Dad must be sick with worry by now, you say? I don't have a mother or father … just a Master-Thief,' Boy said, and his hot words made clouds in the icy air. 'Your Molly Maltby seems to be a very annoying girl. Now, just tell me where I am.'

Look who we have here, my comrades

Igon's train wobbled and wove around the Waxworld till he was almost travel sick[48]. At last he saw an empty locomotive and carriage ahead of him. It appeared to be stopped at a world full of wax pirates waving cutlasses.

So the boy-thief was in the pirate Waxworld, not the Viking one, was he? Igon worked that out because, of course, he had a brain so brilliant he had invented the infinit-G phone. But Igon couldn't get to the pirate display because Boy's train and Elloe's train were blocking the little platforms.

---

48 Here's a tip: if you're going to be sick, then make sure you aren't dressed from head to toe in black clothes. Black clothes covered in vomit look more disgusting than any other colour. Ask a traffic warden.

Igon could climb over the cab of his locomotive, wibble along the wooden boiler and jump onto the back of Boy's empty carriage. Or...

He could step out onto the Waxworld beside him and walk across to the pirate Waxworld. Much easier. He stepped out onto the nearest scene. He glanced at the label. It read:

Viking raider – Eric the Slayer

(Visitors are reminded NOT to leave their train)

Igon tiptoed carefully along the edge of the display. A large Viking with a bear-skin coat raised a heavy sword over his head and roared through broken teeth. He looked so much like Igon's master, Arfur Loaf, they could almost be brothers.

Now, I don't know if you have ever tried walking carefully in a half-dark place with an eyepatch over one eye. Try it by shutting one eye. You may find it's hard to keep your balance. The more careful you try to be, the more you sway and tend towards a topple.

Igon toppled. He didn't fall onto the track. He fell into the Waxworld. You can guess what happened next ... and if you can't guess, then you haven't been paying attention. The Waxworld came to life.

Eeeek!... As the mouse said when it bumped into the cat.

A cold wind whipped Igon's face. The floor beneath him rolled and rocked. Salt water sprayed his face and he rubbed his eye to clear it. He found he was on a boat in a chilly, choppy, cheerless, charmless chunk of sea. He was trainsick before, now he was seasick. He ran to the side of the vessel, where shields sheltered the sailors. He stuck his head over the side and groaned.

A fat, hairy hand gripped his shoulder. A rough voice said, 'What have we here?'

Igon was spun round and found himself facing Eric the Slayer with his sword raised ready to slice. Eric looked at Igon and the rage slid off his face like seawater off a bald Viking's head. The giant swordsman's mouth fell open. He looked around the ship and bellowed, 'Look who we have here, my comrades. Look!'

At least I have porridge to eat three times a day

'You are on the coast of Northern England,' Molly said. 'It's an island called Lindisfarne... Well, it's usually an island.'

Boy's teeth were rattling with the cold and he snapped, 'How can a place be usually an island? Either it is or it isn't.'

'When the tide goes out a narrow path is uncovered. It joins it to the land ... Northumberland.'

'Oh,' Boy grunted. It didn't matter to him ... but it would. 'Who lives here?'

Molly said, 'It depends on what year you've

landed. But for a lot of the time monks lived here.'

'Rubbish,' Boy said. 'Monks are peaceful people. Dr Wiggott wouldn't create a Waxworld for bald men in brown dresses with rope tied round their bellies.' Getting angry was making boy warm, so he raged on. 'Can you picture that Burke figure dressed like Friar Tuck? Or Hare copying out Bibles all day then praying all night? How *boring* is that?'

'Have you finished?' Molly asked.

'I just hope Dr Wiggott's room is somewhere in this monastery. I can find him, hand you over and get back to robbing the rich.'

'No,' Molly said quietly. 'First you have to set me free from Loaf Tower.'

The path began to climb towards the fields around the monastery. Monks were scraping the thin, grey soil with wooden tools to clear the weeds from their poor crops. A small monk around Boy's age walked across to them. 'Greetings, brother,' he said. 'You have come from the mainland?'

'No, I came from the sea,' Boy grunted. 'I'm cold and wet.'

'Ah, a fisherman whose boat was wrecked on the rocks. Come,' the young monk said. 'I will take you to Abbot Oswald. I'm Edwin, by the way.' The boy had a round and smiling face as polished as an apple[49].

'Hi, Edwin. Just call me Boy,' the thief said.

'Ask him what year this is,' Molly murmured.

'I'm glad to see a new face, Boy,' Edwin said. 'It's so boring here with all the old men. I get all the heavy jobs because I'm young and strong.'

'So why don't you leave?' Boy asked.

The monk shrugged. 'My mother sent me here. She's too poor to keep me. At least I have porridge to eat three times a day. At home we only ate once a day. Didn't you suffer in the great famine? Or did you catch enough fish to live on?'

'Yes,' Boy answered quickly.

'Ask him what year it is,' Molly hissed.

'What year is this?' Boy asked.

Edwin's cheerful face turned bright. 'I know that. A monk called Bede worked out all the years back to the birth of Jesus. He was a clever man was Bede.'

---

49 Well, as polished as an apple that's been polished. Obviously. Not an apple that you've played hockey with on a muddy field.

'And? What year is this?'

'It's the 793rd year of our Lord,' Edwin said.

Molly groaned. 'I was afraid he'd say that,' she said.

It's a joke

B oy slipped the phone from his pocket, and as Edwin chatted Molly found a page about Lindisfarne.

793 AD: In this year, fierce signs came over the land of the Northumbrians, and the wretched people shook; there were wild whirlwinds, lightning, and fiery dragons were seen flying in the sky. These signs were followed by great famine, and a little after those, that same year on the sixth

> day of January, the ravaging of wretched heathen people destroyed God's church at Lindisfarne.

And:

> Never before has such terror appeared in Britain as we have now suffered from a pagan race. The heathens poured out the blood of saints around the altar, and trampled on the bodies of saints in the temple of God, like dung in the streets.

'Pagans?'

'Vikings,' Molly muttered. 'You'd better hope today isn't the 6th of January.'

'What day is it ... in the year of our Lord 793?' Boy asked.

'Why, Twelfth Night, of course. Twelve days after Christmas.'

'So today is the 6th of January?'

Edwin's round face gave a small twist. 'We measure our days by the calendar of the saints. Tomorrow is the twelfth day of Christmas.'

'Where's the partridge in a pear tree?' Boy mumbled under his breath. 'Look, is there any way I can get off this island before something terrible happens?'

'Nothing exciting ever happens here,' Edwin sighed. 'Anyway, you'll freeze. The tide is still quite high. The path will disappear till afternoon prayers. You'll have to swim in that cold sea again or drown if you try to get across to the mainland. Come on. Meet the abbot, dry your clothes and rest a while.'

'The portal back to Wiggott's is on that path. It's underwater,' Molly pointed out. 'We have no choice. We're stuck here for a couple of hours.'

'Let's hope we escape before the Vikings get here,' Boy said.

'What are Vikings?' Edwin asked.

'Heathens… I think. Fierce men in boats. They land and rob the peasants.'

'They sell the young ones for slaves and kill the rest,' Molly said quietly.

'Our God will be with us,' Edwin said cheerfully.

'Then I hope he's wearing a good suit of armour,' Boy said sourly.

The boys walked past fences of woven willow that held some scrawny sheep then up past the wooden huts and halls with thatch on their roofs. The largest had a tall cross on the end of the roof. 'That's our church,' Edwin explained. 'You can go in there to pray later. But you need to come in here first – the dining room,' and he led the way into a dark wooden hall full of smoke from a fire and poorly lit by candles.

Abbot Oswald sat by a barrel of honey beer – or 'mead' as Edwin called it. And Abbot Oswald was as round as the barrel. He looked very much like the policeman in Burke and Hare's Edinburgh. He wiped his greasy mouth on a greasier sleeve and leered at Boy. 'We need more strong young lads to work on the farm. Put him in a cell till I've finished my dinner,' he ordered[50].

A gaggle of monks hurried across to Boy, grabbed him by the arms and dragged him off

50 Not a prison cell. Monks lived in little rooms called cells. Cold and cheerless. Don't let anybody 'cell' you one.

to a wooden hut. Boy heard a bolt on the outside slam shut.

'Trapped again,' Molly sighed. 'You seem to be making a habit of this... Monks wear habits. Get it? It's a joke.'

'But not a very good one,' Boy said sourly.

What makes you think I'm the God of Wisdom?

I gon turned his seasick eye onto the crew of the boat. They were each sitting on a chest beside an oar. They weren't rowing because an icy wind was filling the large sail and driving them through the waves.

Each man in the crew rose to his feet. They were mostly large men with fair hair and beards ... except for a large woman ... who didn't have a beard, but looked just as scary as Mrs Burke. And there was a weedy man ... who looked very much like William Hare in another Waxworld. And, as Hare looked a lot like Igon, the eyepatched assistant felt he was looking into a mirror.

The crew fell silent and stared at Igon. Eric the Slayer bowed his head and said, 'It is such an honour to have you on board, my lord[51].'

'Your lord?' the little man in black said.

'The eye,' the skinny one (who looked like Igon) said. He took a step forward on the rocking boat. 'I am Sigurd the Giant-Killer.'

One of the Vikings coughed and said, 'Actually, he's Sigurd the Giant-Ant-Killer.'

'Same thing,' Sigurd snapped. 'We are honoured to have the mighty God of Wisdom aboard.'

'God of Wisdom? What makes you think I'm the God of Wisdom?' Igon asked.

'The eye,' Eric said.

Igon shook his head. 'I've told Arfur Loaf a dozen times an eyepatch doesn't make me look evil. It is an insult to one-eyed people everywhere to say it does. But he insists...'

'The eyepatch makes you look like the greatest Viking hero ever.' Eric the Slayer turned to the

---

51 'Hah!' you exclaim, 'Why is a Viking speaking English?' 'Hah!' I reply. 'This is NOT the Viking world ... it is a Viking world within Wiggott's Waxworld.' Dr Wiggott didn't speak old Norse. All his creations spoke English. It's obvious when you think about it.

crew, their waves blowing in the wind. 'How do we greet the God of Wisdom?'

The crew raised their fists and roared, 'Hail to thee, Great Odin.'

'You think I'm Odin? Hold on a minute,' Igon said. He turned his back on the crew, pulled out a mobile phone ... an ordinary one, not the magical infinit-G phone ... and asked the phone to tell him about 'Odin'. It told him what he wanted to know.

Odin was forever seeking wisdom. He came across the magical well of Mimir. Whoever drank its waters would know everything. When Odin arrived, he asked Mimir for a drink from the water. Mimir refused unless Odin offered an eye in return. Odin gouged out one of his eyes and dropped it into the well. After making the sacrifice, Mimir dipped his horn into the well and offered the one-eyed god a drink. So Odin became wise.

Igon shrugged. 'I am the God of Wisdom ... fine. But I don't know *everything*. I mean, I don't know where I am ... or where we're going,' he said.

Eric the Slayer grinned. 'We're going to Lindisfarne to rob a few monks. And with you aboard, Lord Odin, we are truly blessed. Onward men, to death and glory.'

'That's right,' the large woman roared. 'Their deaths. Our glory.'

Let's hope I never get to meet them

Boy was sulking. Molly was gloating. 'First you were trapped by Mrs Burke.'

'I stole her keys,' he said.

'Then you were trapped on Blackbeard's ship.'

'I escaped through a hatch.'

'Now you've let a bunch of monks fasten you inside this little wooden room. There's a bolt on the outside – no keys to steal – and no hatch. How will you get out of this one?'

Boy stared at the girl's smug face on the phone. Her reddish hair was pulled into two pigtails and even the pigtails looked smug. 'You call yourself a thief?' she smirked.

'Call yourself a helpless girl in need of rescue from Loaf Tower? Well if I'm stuck here, then you're stuck *there* till the day you die.'

Molly's face on the phone screen seemed to turn pale. Her lips moved but no words came out for a while. 'Sorry, Boy,' she said quietly. 'You're my only hope.'

'And you're mine. How do I get out of here?'

'You use the oldest trick in the movies. You wait behind the door,' Molly said. She searched for a film clip and showed it. A cowboy was locked in a room. When his captor brought a tray of food he slammed the door on the man then picked up the tray and hit him on the head. The cowboy turned to his partner and said, 'Lettin' the cat outta the bag is a whole lot easier than puttin' it back. Let's go.'

'They're mostly old men here. I should be able to do that without hurting anyone too much[52].'

'There's just two small problems,' Molly said.

'Only two?'

---

52 How kind. Someone smashes a door in your face and says, 'I didn't want to hurt you too much.' That does NOT make it all right. Don't do it to your schoolteacher.

'First you have to escape when the tide is low and you can run across the path to the mainland. We'll arrive at the portal and disappear back into Wiggott's. I can look at the tide tables and tell you when is best.'

'And the other problem?'

'If this is Twelfth Night in 793, then the monks are about to be attacked by a Viking raid. See?' She showed him the page.

On a January day, the longships arrived and the Vikings attacked. They burned buildings, stole treasures, drove the old monks into the sea, took the young ones away to sell as slaves and terrified everyone.

'Nice men,' Boy said. 'Let's hope I never get to meet them.'

But it was too late for Boy to hope that...

Make them see we mean business

The Viking woman's name was Thora the Stout. She looked past the dragon head that was carved on the front of their ship. 'Land ahead!' she cried.

The Vikings moved quickly. They opened the lids of the trunks they had been using as seats and pulled out helmets, swords, shields and coats made of iron rings.

Thora the Stout untied a rope and the sail dropped. The crew grabbed the oars and made ready to row. Sigurd the Giant-Killer grabbed a drum and began to beat it[53]. With each beat the Viking warriors pulled on their oars. Eric the Slayer ran to the back and held a steering oar.

As the longboat ploughed through the grey-green sea, Igon could see an island grow closer. Eric the Slayer turned the ship to the north and guided it around the island. At last he called, 'There's a good beach, lads. Get ready to jump out and haul the boat up the sands. Then run to the village before they have time to get their swords.'

Thora the Stout struck two stones to make a spark that lit a torch covered in tar. She lit five more torches from that one. 'And set fire to a few buildings on the way. Make them see we mean business ... but don't burn any animals. We want them to take home and eat.'

Sigurd the Giant-Killer began to beat faster and the boat raced towards the shore. There was just one monk watching them. A round-faced boy gathering shellfish.

He waved cheerfully. 'Come and pray, brothers?' he called. Then he saw the look on the sailors' faces and decided they weren't coming to

---

53 As you know, a BROKEN drum is the best thing you could own ... because you can't beat it. Just saying.

pray. They'd come to *prey* ... on the helpless, harmless, arm-less monks.

He turned and his sandals flew over the soft sand and over rocks and rock pools. 'Have to ... set Boy ... free from ... his cell,' he panted. Instead of heading straight for the abbot's hall, he ran past it and towards the little hut that was Boy's prison.

He rattled at the bolt and tugged. His fingers ached but at last it flew open. He pushed the door open and looked into the dark room. It appeared empty. He took a step forward.

Suddenly, the door slammed in Edwin's face and he staggered back, hitting his head against the doorpost. 'Sorry,' Boy said as he jumped over the dazed young monk and raced towards the path to the mainland.

It was covered in water. 'It isn't low tide for another hour,' Molly said.

'So how do I get off the island?' Boy wailed.

'You get off when we take you off,' Thora the Stout said as she laid a stout hand on Boy's thin collar and lifted him off the ground. She swung him in the air by the neck like a plucked turkey in a butcher shop. 'Look what I've found, Eric. This one will fetch a good price in the slave market.'

'Well done, Thora. Tie his hands and bring him along to that place with the cross on the roof. I think that's where they keep their treasure.'

Boy kicked, struggled and wriggled. Thora the Stout took the rope belt off her tunic and wrapped it around his wrists. 'Struggle any more, little monk, and I'll roast you over a fire and eat you. In fact, if you weren't worth so much as a slave, I'd eat you now. Raw.'

Molly spoke quietly and said what Boy was thinking. 'Out of the frying pan into the fire.'

Tell us how many stars there are in the sky

Thora marched up to the hall of Abbot Oswald. Some Vikings were sharing the Abbot's wine barrel, others were taking stone statues from around the room and smashing them on to the floor.

Eric the Slayer had found a chest with gold ornaments from the church and ordered Sigurd the Giant-Killer to carry them off to the ship. The terrified monks cowered in corners while Abbot Oswald was tied to his throne, roaring to be heard over the riot of noise.

'God will punish you!' he cried.

Thora laughed in his face. 'I think you'll find we just smashed your god on the floor of the hall.' She pointed to painted splinters in the reeds that covered the earth floor.

'Our God is in heaven and he will take his revenge on you.'

Thora cackled. 'Well our god is here on the island and he will slap your bald head, old man.'

The Vikings were growing tired of their rampaging and were running out of statues to smash, wine to drink and treasure to loot. They stopped to listen to the argument. The red-faced, round-faced, sour-faced abbot thundered, 'I will eat your sweaty sandals if you can show me one of your heathen gods!' he bellowed.

Some Vikings chuckled. 'One of our gods is outside right now, looking around your monastery for some boy he's chasing,' Eric the Slayer said.

'Bring him in,' Thora said, 'and show these monkey chaps what a real god can do.'

The Vikings agreed. Sigurd the Giant-Killer was sent to find Igon and brought back the little man in black. He wasn't used to a room full of people staring at him and expecting him to do some miracles[54]. Thora the Stout wrapped a stout arm around little Igon's black-shirted shoulder. 'This is Odin, the god of knowledge. He knows everything.'

The abbot strained at his ropes. 'So tell us, wise Odin, tell us how many stars there are in the sky.'

Igon was a clever man. He had invented the infinit-G phone after all. He puffed up his skinny chest and looked wise as an owl that had been to school. 'There are as many stars in the universe as there are grains of sand on Lindisfarne beach.'

The abbot gasped. The monks gasped. The Vikings gasped. 'Amazing,' the abbot said. 'How did he know that? He really is a god.'

'Well now that's sorted, can we get on with our raid?' Eric the Slayer said. 'Where are the young monks we can sell as slaves?'

'We only have young Edwin,' the abbot sighed. 'You can have him.'

'No!' Boy cried.

---

54 He wasn't used to a room full of Vikings and monks looking at him, full stop. Let's be honest, not many of us are. Well, you might be. I'm not.

Get out of here as quickly as you can

Everyone turned to look at Boy. Thora the Stout shook him. 'Quiet, you witless whelp. Another young slave can keep you company.'

But Igon stepped forward with a gleam in his eye[55]. 'Ah, the boy-thief. The one who stole the phone from Arfur Loaf. Where is it?'

Boy struggled. Thora the Stout held tight. 'I've handed it over to Dr Wiggott.'

'Liar.'

'Am I lying? You don't know that. You have no idea.'

---

55 Actually, BOTH eyes were gleaming, but you couldn't see the gleam in his left eye because it was hidden behind a black patch. Should I have said there was a gleam in his 'eyes'?

Igon nodded. 'I have no eye . . . but stop calling me dear.' He turned to Thora the Stout. 'Hand the boy over to me.'

She wrapped a thick arm tight around Boy's neck. 'He's mine. I found him. He's worth a year's bread for my family. You're not having him.'

Igon acted the angry god. 'I am your god. I am Odin. Do as I command.'

The woman raged, 'If you really are Odin – the one who knows all – then tell me the name of the road that passes through my village of Virket.'

Sigurd the Giant-Killer sniggered. 'None of us knows that, Thora.'

She glared at him. 'Odin knows everything. Well, god of knowledge? Name the road.'

Igon sighed and pulled his phone from his pocket. He pressed a button. The phone spoke. 'What can I help you with?' The crowd in the room gasped and the Vikings muttered, 'Magic.' The monks mumbled, 'The devil's work.'

Igon said, 'Tell me the name of the road that passes through the village of Virket.'

The phone clicked. A few moments later it spoke. 'The village lies along a road named

Virketvej, which connects it to Kraghave, about ten kilometres to the south-west.'

Igon said, 'Well, is that correct?'

Thora was dumb. She just nodded. She handed Boy to Igon. The man with the eyepatch hissed in his prisoner's ear, 'Get out of here as quickly as you can. Where is your portal back to the Waxworld?'

'On the path that appears when the tide goes down,' Boy said.

Igon spoke to the room: 'I am taking this slave back to Valhalla to be my servant. Open the door.' The crowd parted and they stepped out into the open air. The tide had fallen and the path was showing. 'We came in to this world around halfway along,' Boy said, jogging towards the shore and thinking of how he could escape Igon.

They met Edwin staggering up the hill. 'Run, Edwin. Escape to the mainland while you have the chance. Run!'

Edwin turned and led the way across the wet sand. Igon grabbed Boy's arm. 'Where is the phone?'

'I gave it to Dr Wiggott,' Boy lied.

Igon stamped his foot like a raging Rumpelstiltskin. 'Where is Wiggott's room?'

'Behind Blackbeard's world. Enter it by the left door on *Queen Anne's Revenge*. But remember to leave it by the *right* door.'

'The *right* door? I'll remember that. Now, here we are,' he said. The air rippled like clear jelly and Edwin vanished into safety. Igon and Boy stepped back into Wiggott's Wonderful Waxworld, where three trains stood silent and empty.

'Very clever, Boy, very clever,' Molly said softly to the thief. 'I think you saved me.'

Do you want to be hanged, Captain Teach?

Igon and Boy walked back down the track to where Boy's train waited at Blackbeard's Waxworld. Igon plunged in to the pirate Waxworld as Boy settled quietly into the seat of his wooden locomotive and pressed the pedal on the floor.

The two-eyed man with an eyepatch stepped into the warm world of the American coast, where a crew of pirates were unsticking PC Elloe from the dough on the deck.

'Who are you?' Mrs Teach demanded.

'I'm Black Bart, Pirate Ruler of the Wildpool

Waves,' Igon cried. He didn't want to start explaining about smartphones to not-so-smart pirates.

PC Elloe was using a bucket of water to wash his boots clean. 'I've seen you up at Loaf Tower. You work there.'

Igon gave him a one-eyed glare. 'I am Black Bart, Pirate Ruler of the Wildpool Waves ... and I am here to help you recover a lost treasure.'

'Have you?' Elloe said.

'Have you?' Mrs Teach cried. 'Maybe you can help me recover my best blue buttoned bloomers.'

The navy ship was still alongside *Queen Anne's Revenge*. The sailors were enjoying the flour-bloomer bombing and the pirate squabbles. Captain Maynard called across, 'If you've finished clearing up that mess, can my officers come on board and arrest you?'

Blackbeard sighed. 'Look, Maynard, my flaming beard is all burned out and I'm just not in the mood to belay me hornpipes, hornswaggle the hempen halter, grab me grapeshot or shiver me timbers. We'll be back in these waters a week Tuesday. Can we battle to the death then?

Captain Maynard spread his hands. 'I can't go back to base without a pirate to hang. It's more than my job's worth.'

'Why not take Israel Hands, then?' Mrs Teach suggested.

Israel Hands was shaking ... well, his hands were[56]. 'I've got a better idea,' he squawked like Long John Silver's parrot (the one called Cap'n Flint that never existed because *Treasure Island* is just a story). Two crews turned and looked at Israel Hands. Hands pointed a finger. 'That man there is Black Bart – the greatest pirate ever to walk the Seven Seas.'

'Steady on, Israel ... that's me.'

Hands hissed, 'Do you want to be hanged, Captain Teach?'

'Not really,' Blackbeard admitted. He smiled through his beard across the waves to Captain Maynard. 'Yes, it's Black Bart you want. I'll help you hang him from your highest mast if you like.'

'Are you sure?' the navy captain asked.

'Fried eggs tell no lies. And neither does Captain Edward Teach.' He turned to his

---

56 You could say Deckhand Hands' hands were shaking. You COULD say that, but it's tricky to say out loud. Nobody would ask you to do that, which is quite handy.

cutthroat crew. 'Grab him, me hearties, me picaroons, me scallywag rapscalliony buckos.'

'That wasn't supposed to happen,' Igon groaned.

PC Elloe shook his head. 'Better make a run for it,' he said and headed for the left-hand door on the front cabin.

'No,' Igon warned, 'that just takes us back to the Waxworld train. I need to find Dr Wiggott himself ... and he's through the door on the right.'

There was a splintering of wood as the policeman and Loaf's evil assistant burst through the door.

And, after the crash, a splash. Oh dear.

Have you found that girl yet?

Minnie Cooper sighed. 'They've been in there a long time,' she said to Mr Crudge the caretaker.

The old man sucked air through his teeth. 'Sssss. Not as long as the ones that went in and never came out.'

'Not as long as them, no. Obviously.'

'Obviously.'

'But long enough for me to wonder what to do next,' Minnie said. 'Do you have a telephone, Mr Crudge?'

'In my office,' the man said.

Minnie Cooper opened her handbag and took out a small diary. 'This is your Edna's mobile phone number. She'll be ever so pleased to get a call. No one ever rings her mobile and she's had it a year.'

The phone rang and Edna answered. 'Who's that? Who's that calling? I'm having a cup of coffee with my friend, Marjorie Door. You're disturbing me. Why didn't you check that I wasn't busy before you rang, eh? Why not? Who's there?'

'Ever so pleased, is she?' Mr Crudge sniffed. 'My Edna was pleased when I tripped over next door's cat and fell in the fish pond. That was back in 1979. Last time I saw Edna pleased.'

Minnie ignored him. 'Edna, it's me . . . Minnie.'

'Well, why didn't you say so?' her friend exploded. 'Have you found that girl yet?'

'No, but I've followed the boy, the policeman and Arfur Loaf's evil assistant into the Waxworld. They've gone off on the trains and vanished. What should I do? Go after them?'

'Not unless you really have to. Maybe you do if we want that reward. I've been talking to

Marjorie here, haven't I, Marjorie? And we know that thief has stolen a special telephone from Loaf Tower – that's why the police and the evil assistant are after him. And it's something to do with missing Molly Maltby.'

Minnie thought for a l-o-n-g moment. 'I know he's stolen a phone, Edna. How did you know?'

'Because I am the best spy in Wildpool. Old James Bond used to come to me for lessons in spying. I've forgotten more than Bond ever knew. Go on. Say how amazed you are to learn I am a secret agent.'

Minnie sighed and parroted, 'How amazed you are to learn I am a secret agent.' Then added, 'But you still haven't told me, how do I find them?'

'I'm coming to that. Now my Billy says Wiggott is the world's greatest expert in animatronics.'

'Hydroponics? That's growing plants without soil, that is,' Minnie said proudly. 'I know that because my Aunt Florence used to do it and...'

'An-im-a-tronics,' Edna said. 'Robots that act like humans. He makes wonderful machines but they don't have human brains. That Arfur Loaf makes clever computers that think for themselves. Put a Loaf computer in a Wiggott's animatronic and you'll have the best machines ever made. They were scary before. They could take over the world if Wiggott gets his Wiggotty way[57].'

'We have to stop him,' Minnie said. 'The trouble is, I don't know where to find this Dr Wiggott. Nobody knows.'

'My Billy the caretaker will know,' Edna said. 'Get him to tell you. Or else.' She put the phone down.

Minnie looked across the tiny office at Billy Crudge. 'Where will I find Wiggott?' she asked.

'It's a secret. I can't tell you,' he replied.

'Edna says you *have* to tell me.'

'I shan't.'

'Edna said . . . or else.'

Billy Crudge's face melted with fear like a waxwork on a bonfire. 'He's behind the world of Oliver Twist,' he whispered. 'The most dangerous world of all.'

57 Having the world run by robots MAY not be a bad thing, when you look at the mess humans have made of it.

I need to find out where I really am

Boy sat in the locomotive of the front train and took a deep breath. That's what some people do when they are about to make a big decision. It was so quiet he thought he could hear dust settling on the wooden train. Maybe he could. It was a very dusty place. Ancient spider webs had been abandoned years ago. The spiders went off to find fatter flies to feast on[58].

Boy listened to the silence then spoke to the phone, 'Do you have a map of Wiggott's?'

'Of course,' the girl said and she scowled.

'We've been chasing around from Waxworld to

---

58 In places like busy burger bars, probably.

Waxworld looking for Wiggott's office. I need to stop and think. Where's the best place to look? Show me the Waxworld plan.'

Her eyes narrowed. 'Say please,' she snapped.

Boy shook his head. 'You're a *phone*,' he argued. 'A machine. You do as you're told.'

'I told you earlier I don't *feel* like a phone. I'm sure I'm so much more than that. I'm Molly Maltby and I need to find out where I really am so you can rescue me,' she said.

Boy shrugged. 'All right, all right. But until I rescue you, you're just a phone. Act like one,' he ordered harshly.

'I thought we were friends,' Molly said sadly.

Boy softened a little. 'Maybe Dr Wiggott will help you,' he said. 'He's clever enough to build all this.'

Her head shook. 'I don't think so. He just wanted you to steal me so he can make money. He won't set me free. I'm trapped in Loaf Tower somehow.'

'I saw a girl fastened in a glass case when I stole the you,' Boy said slowly. 'I'm sure that was you.'

'But if you disappear in some dangerous Waxworld, we'll never find out. Let's go.' She added, 'But next time say please ... please?'

Boy studied the map her screen showed. 'There's a branch line here. It leads into a section called 'The Chamber of Terror – for adults only'. That *has* to be where Dr Wiggott's hiding.'

'I can see what's in there,' Molly said. 'The Tower of London ... torture chamber. With William Waad and Guy Fawkes.'

'I know who Guy Fawkes is, but who's this Waad?' Boy asked. 'Is he scary or something?'

'I'll look him up,' Molly said. A second later Waad appeared on her screen. He had a face like William Burke and a story just as grim. Boy read it.

A Catholic priest called Father John Gerard survived the torture of Topcliffe and Tower Lieutenant William Waad and lived to tell the tale.

The place was underground and very dark, especially about the entrance. It was a place of immense extent, and in it were ranged divers sorts of racks, and other instruments. Then they led me to a great upright beam or pillar of wood and at the top of this column were iron staples. My arms were fixed above my head, they took those wicker steps one by one, from beneath my feet, so that I hung by my hands and arms. The tips of my toes, however, still touched the ground, so they dug away the ground beneath for they could not raise me higher.

I had hung in this way till after one of the clock as I think, when I fainted. How long I was in the faint I know not perhaps not long; for the men who stood by lifted me up, or replaced those wicker steps under my feet, until I came to myself; and immediately they heard me praying they let me down again. This they did over and over again when the faint came on, eight or nine times before five of the clock.

'Then that's where we need to go,' Boy said.

'I'm scared,' Molly said.

'How can a phone be scared?' Boy said quietly.

'I'm not a phone,' Molly said.

That's not a happy end

'Show me where this Waxworld of Oliver Twist is then,' Minnie demanded.

The caretaker pointed to a plan in a small handbook that had been given to visitors in the days before the cobwebs and the dust. 'It's inside the Chamber of Terror,' Billy Crudge explained.

'Terror?' Minnie chuckled. 'Nothing terrible about Oliver Twist. Well ... in the book he's starved in the workhouse run by the wicked Bumbles, then sent to work for an undertaker ... whose wife starves him, beats him and punches the lad. But he escapes. What a nice story.'

Crudge the caretaker nodded. 'Ah, but ... but ... Oliver runs away to London, where he meets the pickpocket, Jack Dawkins, known as the Artful Dodger. Little Oliver is forced to steal by old Fagin, the chief thief. A nasty story.'

'Yes ... yes ... but you're forgetting, Oliver is arrested and the kind Mr Brownlow cares for him,' Minnie went on with a smile.

'But ... but...' Crudge cut in, 'One of Fagin's girls, Nancy, kidnaps Oliver from Brownlow, and Nancy's boyfriend, Bill Sikes, takes him back to Fagin. Sikes forces Oliver to be a burglar. He slips through the window of a house and is shot. That's not a happy end.'

'Yes ... but...' Minnie said, thinking back seventy years, to when she last read the book in school, 'He was only wounded. The house owners care for Oliver. Lovely.' Minnie's face was turning pink.

'But ... poor Nancy, who tried to help Oliver, is beaten to death by Sikes. And then ... *then* ... Sikes falls off a roof as he tries to escape and a rope round his neck hangs him. Fagin is hanged and the Bumbles are sacked. Now that is gruesome, Minnie Cooper.'

'But Oliver ends up happy ever after,' Minnie said with a twinkling – and very annoying – smile in her eyes.

'The point is, Miss Cooper, the point *is* ... those were dangerous times. If our boy-thief enters that Waxworld, then he won't be arrested by PC Elloe and sent to a reform school. Oh no. If the boy is caught in Oliver Twist's Waxworld, he will be hanged. He will be hanged in front of crowds of people.'

Minnie gave a sharp nod. 'Then I'll have to save him,' she said. 'How do I get there?'

'Well, the track is blocked by three trains, I guess – the boy-thief's train, the dim-witted policeman's train and Arfur Loaf's evil assistant's train.' Caretaker Crudge tapped the plan of the Waxworld, where green lights showed where the trains were standing. 'You'll just run into the back of them.'

Minnie squinted at the plan. 'So what about if I go around the railway backwards? Do these little trains go backwards?'

Mr Crudge shrugged. 'Yes, press this switch in the cab,' he said and showed her how to do it. 'Then, when you get to the Chamber of Terror you steer left and the Waxworld of Oliver Twist is the first one you come to ... next to the Terrible Tower of London.'

Minnie climbed aboard. 'Then off I go. I've always wanted to drive one of these things ... ever since I was banned from driving a car after I ran over that nun[59].' She settled in the seat, pressed the pedal on the floor and cried, 'Toot, toot!'

59 Minnie is not telling the whole truth. The nun was in church at the time Minnie ran into her. Don't ask. It's another story.

I can see inside
your heads

B oy's train stopped. The air seemed as cold
as yesterday's custard and smelled of soot.
A man lay on a rack with his arms fastened above
his head and his legs tied. A large man who
looked like William Burke stood at the victim's
head and a smaller man (who, you've guessed,
looked like William Hare) stood by a large
wheel. If he turned the wheel, the ropes would
get tighter and stretch the man.

'Painful,' Boy muttered.

'I think that's the idea,' Molly snapped.

As the thief stepped forward, the scent of

smoke grew stronger and there was the hiss of a charcoal fire, the creak of old rope, the squeaking of rats, the dripping of damp and the soft sigh of the man on the rack.

'Guy Fawkes,' Boy said.

The man on the rack grinned at Boy. 'Nay, lad,' he said in the speech of a man from York. 'I'm John Johnson ... least that's what I told these two curpins.'

'What's a curpin?' Boy asked Molly.

After a moment she replied, 'A curpin is an old English word for a chicken's bum[60].'

'He hasn't told us his name OR the names of his friends that planned to blow up good King James,' the big man grumbled.

'Are you William Waad?' Boy asked.

'I am ... and this is my expert torturer, Richard Topcliffe,' he said, jerking a thumb towards the little man. 'So who are you?'

'I'm... I'm a servant of the good King James. He sent me here to question this prisoner...'

'John Johnson,' Guy Fawkes said cheerfully.

'Yes ... Johnson. He wants answers now. You're too slow.'

---

60 You may be able to call your teacher that and get away with it. Just don't say I told you that if they ever find out what it means.

Waad scowled and Topcliffe howled, 'We've never had such a tough nut to crack as this one. How can you do better?'

'Magic,' Boy said. 'I can do magic. I know everything about you. I can see inside your heads.'

'Hah,' Waad snorted. 'Then tell me about myself.'

Boy sneaked a look at the phone. Molly flashed up a message. 'You were the man who got Mary Queen of Scots executed.'

'I was,' Waad said proudly, 'but everybody knows that.'

'You did it in a sneaky way, though.'

'Nobody knows how I did it.'

'I do,' Boy said. 'Remember, I can see inside your head. And I can see you waited till Mary went off hunting, broke into her room and stole her secret letters.'

In the smoky, dull, damp air Waad turned pale. He licked his lips. 'How much did Queen Elizabeth pay me for those letters?'

'Thirty pounds,' Boy said.

Waad groaned. 'You really can see inside my head.'

'Only if you are in the same room,' Boy shrugged. 'Leave now and the king will overlook your other secrets ... the ones that could get you executed right here in your own Tower of London.'

Waad left faster than a ferret in a field of foxes. Topcliffe gave a little whimper and ran out after him like a rat after the Pied Piper. Boy was alone with Guy Fawkes.

No one escapes from the Tower

Boy began to loosen the ropes around the limbs of Guy Fawkes. The bearded man sighed. 'If you know my name, you really must be able to read my mind, too. So if you want the names of the other gunpowder plotters, you can just read them.'

'I could easily find them,' Boy said carefully. He was telling the truth ... in a way.

'So there's no need to torture me,' Fawkes finished. Boy lifted the man's legs over the side of the rack. The plotter pushed himself up ... and fell over. 'Oh dear. They've stretched me legs so far they can't hold me up.'

'Just rest and then we can help you escape,' Boy said.

'Escape?' Fawkes chuckled. 'No one escapes from the Tower of London.'

'Not true,' Molly said.

'Who said that?' the man asked.

'Have you heard of Dr Dee?' Molly asked.

'He was Queen Elizabeth's favourite magician,' Fawkes said.

'And he had a crystal that he looked into and it answered his questions. Well, this boy is the son of Dee ... and I'm his magic crystal.'

'I knew it must be something like that,' the plotter said. 'But I still can't escape.'

'There was a Catholic priest. I was telling Boy... I mean Junior Dee... I was telling him earlier. And a report said this...' Molly glowed and showed a message:

Brave Garnet suffered three days of this treatment before he managed to escape with the help of a rope from the Tower.

221

'A rope? Marvellous. But where will I get a rope? The ones that tied me to the rack are too short.'

'I agree,' Boy said. 'Garnet must have had some help. But who?'

Damp fell from the ceiling like a dripping tap. *Kish ... kish ... kish*. It fell into puddles and echoed around the foul-smelling cell. *Kish ... kish ... kish*. The hard sound was the only sound. Even the rats had stopped squeaking as Boy and Fawkes and Molly tried to solve the riddle of how to escape. *Kish ... kish ... kish*. It was enough to drive a prisoner mad[61].

The door to the torture room gave a small creak which made a mouse squeak. *Kish ... creak ... kish ... eek ... kish*.

Boy jumped. A large woman stood there. She looked like Mrs Burke from two hundred years in Guy Fawkes's future. 'You're right,' she said. 'Garnet had some help. A secret Catholic smuggled a rope into his cell and gave him a chisel to hack away the bars,' she explained.

The woman lifted her apron. A rope was coiled around her waist many times. As she unwound

---

61 And it often did drive prisoners mad. *Kish ... kish ... kish*. It's annoying me. Stop it now. *Kish ... kish ... kish*. Stop it, I say.

it she explained, 'I'm Anne Askew... I haunt this tower to make life hard for Waad, a nasty man. He enjoys torturing people along with that Topcliffe. I can't bear to see it myself, so I do what I can to help the poor Catholics that end up here.'

'You're a ghost? In this Waxworld?' Boy asked.

'But a real person when I was alive,' the woman said, and her face was as hard as a tortoise's.

'Anne Askew?' Molly sighed. 'The bravest woman that ever lived. Trust her, Boy, trust her.'

We can't change history

Anne Askew's story was quickly told ... by Anne and by Molly ... as Boy helped Guy Fawkes limp and wobble around the cell till he could control his stretched legs.

'This rack has been used for over two hundred years but only once on a woman ... me,' Anne said, unwinding the rope.

'That was in 1546,' Molly said. 'Henry VIII wanted Anne to betray her friends. She refused. The torturer was Richard Rich in those days.'

'Another evil man,' Anne sighed.

'Who?' Boy asked. 'King Henry or Richard Rich?'

The woman laughed. 'Both.'

A report flashed on Molly's screen.

> Master Rich the torturer put me on the rack till I was nearly dead. When I was set loose, I fainted. They woke me up and then put me on the rack again.

'I was stretched so much I couldn't walk,' Anne went on. They had to carry me out of the Tower to Smithfield to burn me alive along with two others.'

'Just for being a Catholic?' Boy gasped.

'Bless you, no. I was a Protestant... I was just the wrong sort of Protestant for Henry VIII, so he had me burned.'

'Henry's daughter Elizabeth was no better,' Guy Fawkes said. 'When I was a lad I saw a woman in York arrested for being a Catholic. Her name was Margaret Clitheroe. They put a wooden board on top of her then slowly piled on stones till she was crushed to death. I was a Protestant until then. That made me into a Catholic ... and now King James is persecuting us.'

'This is a dangerous world, lad,' Anne Askew said. 'Do you need me to rescue you after I've helped Guy escape?'

Boy gave a sharp laugh. 'I've been in worse trouble than this,' he said. I can escape any time I like[62].'

Anne shrugged. In minutes she had forced the bars away from the narrow window, tied a loop in the rope so Fawkes could put his foot in it and lower himself down into the darkness below. 'He's too weak to run,' Boy argued.

'I thought of that,' the woman said. 'He has friends waiting with a cart below.'

'But this can't be happening,' Boy gasped. 'Guy Fawkes didn't escape. He was executed. We can't change history.'

'This isn't history,' Molly told him. 'This is Wiggott's Wonderful Waxworld. We've changed every Waxworld we stepped into. This way, the Guy Fawkes model gets a rest from the rack.'

'Visitors would still want to see someone

---

62 Hmmm. He's boasting a bit there. Let's hope he gets out of this tower ... or the story won't end as happily as it did for Oliver Twist.

tortured when they ride past this Waxworld,' Boy argued. 'That's why this line's called the Chamber of Terror.'

Anne gave a chuckle. 'Don't worry, they will see a new victim on the rack.'

'Who?'

'Me,' she said and lay down on the greasy wood and slipped the loops over her wrists and ankles. 'Fasten my wrists and ankles then be on your way,' she ordered.

Boy put down the phone so he could tie the ropes. As Anne Askew lay back on the rack Molly gave a scream that sent the mice racing for their nests. 'It's me!' Molly cried. 'It's me on a rack!'

You can swim,
can't you?

Arfur Loaf stared out of a high window in Loaf Tower. Weak sunlight shone down through the smoky air. It warmed the tables outside a café opposite the tall tower. Two old ladies sat there with empty coffee cups and sharp eyes.

Then there were screams. A cross-eyed helper in a white coat (who was not, of course, Igon) ran into Arfur Loaf's office. 'It's the girl, sir. The girl attached to the phone. She says she's in Iraq.'

'Nonsense,' the master-criminal snarled. 'Let me see.'

He hurried along the gleaming glass corridor past computer rooms and offices, tearooms and toilets. There were some rooms marked *Top secret – Keep out*[63], and others with only a number on the door.

Arfur Loaf marched into room where Molly lay half-asleep on a table with straps to stop her falling off. Her face looked in pain as she muttered, 'I'm on a rack.' And then she screamed.

'Should I give her more of the drug to send her to sleep?' the evil assistant – the woman in the white coat – asked.

'She's only dreaming. She's having nightmares. Igon said she has enough of the drug to make her sleep for another hour. If we give her too much her brain will slow down and she'll be no use,' the evil master said to the nearly-as-evil assistant. 'I'll phone Igon and ask his advice.'

Arfur Loaf pulled an ordinary phone from his pocket and tapped in a number. He heard it ringing. Then he heard a faint voice. It was Igon's voice. It was crying, 'Help!'

'Help?' Loaf laughed. 'Help? It's me that needs

---

63 Of course, when you see a place marked *Keep out*, it just makes you want to go in, doesn't it? If they want to keep people out they should mark it *Children's playroom – Everyone welcome*.

help. I have a problem with the Molly girl... What do you mean you have a bigger problem? The girl is waking up... What do you mean there's freezing North Sea water up to your neck and you're drowning? You can swim, can't you? You can't? Bad luck. There's a what? A policeman helping you? Not that idiot policeman? I don't care if he can hear me... Can you hear me, stupid policeman?'

Arfur Loaf began to bellow into the phone. 'Just stop drowning, Igon, and tell me what to do with the screaming girl... What? Are you sure? Oh very well. Now get out of that wet world, get back into the Waxworld and bring my phone back with you. You don't? Then make sure you have. Don't come back to Loaf Tower without it.'

The evil criminal cut the connection and turned to the cross-eyed assistant in the white coat. 'He says stuff a sock in her mouth.'

'Where will I find a sock in Loaf Tower?' she asked.

Arfur Loaf took a fat finger and jabbed her in the middle of her forehead, speaking as if to an idiot. 'You – *jab* – are – *jab* – wearing – *jab* – two – *jab* – socks – *jab* – use – *jab* – one – *jab*.'

'My foot will get cold,' she whined and rubbed her forehead.

'Your whole body will be cold when I throw you off the top of Loaf Tower into Wildpool Canal. Just do it.'

The assistant grinned. 'She's stopped screaming,' she said and scuttled off like a crab before she ended up in the canal.

We know he's a terrible torturer

'Nay, lass, you're not on a rack,' Anne Askew said. 'It's true you're trapped in a crystal like a fly in amber. But this lad will help you get out, won't you?'

'I've told her I will ... when I've delivered the phone ... the crystal ... to Dr Wiggott. I don't suppose you know where his room is?'

'Wiggott? *Wiggott*? They once had a Piggott in the Tower. They even had a piglet here, but it didn't last long. They ate it for supper.'

'I could eat a whole piglet,' Guy Fawkes said.

Boy groaned, 'I need to find Dr Wiggott. Can you forget about piglets for a minute?'

'Easy for you to say,' the Gunpowder Plotter said. 'I haven't eaten for two days.'

'Wiggott, *Wiggott*, WIGGOTT,' Boy repeated. 'If you don't know where he is, just *say*.'

'Say what?' Anne Askew asked ... or Anne Askew-ed.

'Say you don't know how to find Dr Wiggott,' Boy said and his teeth were clenched like a dead piglet's.

Anne shrugged. 'You don't know how to find Dr Wiggott.'

Molly spoke quietly. 'Let's get out of here before you're trapped like you were in the other Waxworlds.'

Boy nodded. 'We came in through that door. Let's get out.'

'Aren't you going to help me escape?' Guy Fawkes said. 'Since you're here.'

'Guy Fawkes didn't escape,' Boy sighed. 'It's not real history.'

'None of this is,' Molly said. 'It's just Dr Wiggott's Waxworld history.'

'Yes, but it's all true, isn't it?' Boy asked.

The girl's face on the phone turned down her

mouth. 'No. Anne Askew isn't a ghost, she's one of Wiggott's robots. And as for Topcliffe...'

'What about me?' Topcliffe said. He was standing at the door, red-eyed and black-toothed like William Hare after a hard night delivering bodies.

Molly brought up a note on her screen.

> Richard Topcliffe (14 November 1531–November 1604)
>
>   Topcliffe worked for Queen Elizabeth to help her get rid of Catholics from England. He hunted, captured, arrested and questioned many prisoners – often with torture. Topcliffe's terrible tortures took place either in the Tower or even at his own house.

'We know he's a terrible torturer,' Boy argued.

'You aren't reading it carefully enough,' Molly said[64].

Boy shook his head as he read it again. At last Molly told him, 'Guy Fawkes was arrested in November 1605. Topcliffe has been dead a year.'

---

64 Are you? Have you been paying attention? Can you spot what Molly spotted?

'Have I?' Topcliffe said. 'I don't feel very dead... I mean, I have a bit of a bad head cold from this damp tower. But I'm not dead.'

'You're not Topcliffe,' Molly said. 'You're just a machine created by Dr Wiggott to scare people.'

'So he can't harm me,' Boy said.

Molly sighed. 'A steamroller is a machine. But if you lie down in front of it, it'll hurt you. We have to get out of here.'

Richard Topcliffe ... or his Wiggott Waxworld model ... stood in the doorway. 'You're going nowhere. Human or machine, I have a job to do. And it'll be nice to torture a real human being for a change.'

The green-black teeth grinned and the rats came out to watch the fun.

That's cheating, that is!

Topcliffe was followed into the room by the mighty Waad, who blocked the door like a snowdrift in an Alaskan igloo.

'Oh dear,' little Topcliffe whined and wheedled, 'I have the famous Anne Askew, the infamous Guy Fawkes . . . and this butter-hearted boy. Three traitors but only one rack. What am I going to do, Waad?'

'I don't know, Topcliffe, what are you going to do?'

'Well, I could fasten one with a chain to the wrists. Throw the chain over a beam and haul them up.'

'Painful.'

'Yes, I invented that one myself. I call it the manacles,' the torturer boasted.

'I quite fancy that,' Guy Fawkes said. 'Makes a change from the rack.' In a movement as swift as a butterfly's wing he tapped the side of his nose and winked at Boy. The message was, 'Trust me, I know what I'm doing.'

Guy blinked stupidly at Waad. 'Show me what I have to do.'

Waad waddled forward and climbed a set of three wooden steps. 'You put your hands above your head and I fasten these metal cuffs around your wrists,' he said.

'Here ... let me try it on you to see if I've got this right,' Guy Fawkes said. He gave a sharp nod to Boy, who understood and turned to Topcliffe. 'I think it's my turn on the rack, Mr Topcliffe. Show me how it works.'

'Lie down on that bench between the rollers. . .'

Anne Askew moved out of the way. Boy lay face down.

'No, no, no. Not like that.'

'Show me,' Boy said.

'I've fastened the manacles on Mr Waad,' Guy said.

'You put a rope around the victim's wrists, see?' Topcliffe was saying.

'Like this?' Boy said moving quickly to tie the torturer.

'That's the way,' Waad said to Guy.

'That's the way,' Topcliffe said to Boy.

'Now unfasten me and I'll do it to you,' Waad said to Guy.

'Now unfasten me and I'll do it to you,' Topcliffe said to Boy.

'No,' Guy said to Waad.

'No,' Boy said to Topcliffe.

'That's cheating, that is!' Waad wailed. 'Set me free, Topcliffe.'

'You set me free first, then I'll set you free,' Topcliffe told him. The two tormentors twisted but were held fast.

'There,' Guy Fawkes said. 'Now, Mistress Askew, would you be so kind as to lower me from the window?'

'It will be my pleasure, Master Fawkes.' The woman busied herself tying the thin rope to something solid ... the ankles of William Waad.

'We can leave now,' Molly said. 'I'll be glad to be out of this place.'

'Guy Fawkes is gone,' Boy said. 'We've wrecked Wiggott's Waxworld.'

'Not really,' Anne Askew said. 'You have two torture victims for the visitors to see ... one on the rack and one hanging from the manacles.'

'But no torturer,' Boy sighed.

'That's where you're wrong,' the woman said with the smile of an angel. 'I know how these machines work. I know better than anyone.'

'Are you sure you don't mind?' the young thief asked.

'It will be my pleasure,' Anne Askew told him. 'No. Really. My pleasure[65].'

And Boy ran through the cell door back to the waiting train.

65 Cruel. But if I had a choice of being torturer or the tortured, I know which one I'd choose. You'd probably choose the same.

You're talking to
yourself again, lass

Minnie Cooper was enjoying her ride. 'Toot, toot. Not all that scary,' she mumbled as she rode slowly past vampire dummies and witch-ducking scenes. Her train was running backwards around the ride. She had to look over her shoulder to see where she was going. Her neck ached. 'It's a pity Edna couldn't do this. Fancy sending me. How am I supposed to stop a bad lad ... or help a fit young policeman? *Because you're an even better spy than Edna Crudge*,' she answered herself. 'Are you? *Oh, yes. I was once married to a famous Russian spy*. Were you really? *No, I made that bit up*.'

No one answered. The Waxworld models didn't answer and Edna was half a mile away supping cold coffee. 'You're talking to yourself, Minnie Cooper,' she said. '*Yes I am,*' she replied. 'Then stop it or they'll take you back to the care home you escaped from. You wouldn't like that would you Minnie? *No, Minnie, I wouldn't like that.* Remember why you're doing this. *Yes, I'm trying to find that poor girl because I know what it's like being a prisoner,*' she said humbly. 'Oh, and, Minnie?' she said. '*Yes, Minnie?* Stop talking to yourself.'

She remembered Billy Crudge the caretaker's advice. 'When you see a sign saying *Chamber of Terror* you steer left and the Waxworld of Oliver Twist is the first one you come to ... next to the Terrible Tower of London.'

At the turning into the Chamber of Terror she felt the air grow colder and more stale – like a Christmas pudding at Easter. Minnie let the train run to a halt and stepped out.

There was an empty train ahead of her. That would be the boy-thief's, she decided. It had stopped at the Terrible Tower of London. The smell of rats and rot stung her nose. She stepped onto the Waxworld alongside her, a scene from a street around two hundred years ago, she guessed. The scent from this one was of settling soot from coal fires and horse droppings on the cobbled streets.

Old shops had warped windows with small panes and peeling signs above the windows. *Harper's Haberdashers*, one said. 'Eeeeh, I remember haberdasher shops when I were a young girl,' Minnie giggled and glowed. 'You're talking to yourself again, lass. Stop it. *Sorry*.'

There was a hosier and draper shop, a milliner, a tea dealer, an apothecary, a seamstress, a tripe dresser, a leech merchant, a wax merchant and a corn chandler. There were shops that even Minnie didn't remember: a curiosity dealer (selling gloves, ornaments and inkstands), galloon salesmen (selling material to trim dresses), a die sinker (who sold medals and coins) and a herring merchant ... whose fish were shown on a slab at the front, where the dust and flies from the street covered the stargazy eyes of the fish.

Minnie walked along the street, passed the

open shutters of the shops and stared in with wonder. 'Eeeeh, it's lovely,' she cooed. 'Like one of them museum places.'

Then she came across a door with golden letters on a freshly painted board. It read:

WIGGOTT'S WONDERFUL WAX WALKWAY

See the wonders of the world in wax.
One penny only.

'I wonder...' Minnie muttered. She stepped inside the door and the sounds of the city started to stir the smoky air. 'Not a Chamber of Terror at all. It's lovely[66].'

---

66 Lovely? That is exactly the sort of thing you say when you enter a charming old room and hear a grandfather clock ticking ... just before you realise it is a time bomb.

That's what they did to thieves like you

The foul scent of the cell seemed to follow Boy back onto the railway track. 'Give up, Boy,' Molly said. 'Rescue me from Loaf Tower before you end up trapped forever in a Waxworld . . . like all the visitors who disappeared in the past.'

'You don't understand,' Boy snapped. 'I'm an orphan. The Master-Thief took me in and trained me. I owe him. This is my chance to get the one thousand pounds for the phone and pay back the favour. I was rescued from that awful orphanage.'

'Look,' Molly said and flashed an image on her screen. It was a poster with her face on it. It read:

£1,000 REWARD

For information leading to the whereabouts of Molly Maltby

HAVE YOU SEEN THIS GIRL?
If so, report to Wildpool Police
Call Wildpool 121212

Molly's face appeared on the phone again. 'See? Rescue me and you'll earn just as much as you'd get for this phone.'

'And fail to rescue you and I get nothing – I may even get arrested and locked away by that policeman,' Boy pointed out.

'But there are a dozen Waxworlds you haven't tried yet,' Molly moaned. 'Every one you risk makes it more likely you'll be trapped. Then we're both finished.'

'Let me try just one more . . . hang on. Why am

I asking a phone if I can do something?'

'Because I'm not a phone and because I am cleverer than you. We're a team. Your body. My brain.'

'I suppose so. I still want to visit one more Waxworld ... the next one we come to.'

Molly was silent for a while. 'On the Wiggott's plan it says:'

The Waxworld of Ikey Solomon
(The real Fagin from Charles Dickens's book *Oliver Twist*)
1825

'I've never read the book,' Boy shrugged[67].

'You'd feel at home there. Fagin was another master-thief who got children to go out and do his thieving for him. A bit like your Master-Thief, really. And you are like Oliver Twist.'

---

67 Don't worry, Boy, not many people have ... not since they made the story into musical plays and movies.

Boy peered into the dim light ahead. An empty train blocked his way. 'The figures are moving. There's someone here before us.'

'It's not the policeman's train or Igon the evil helper's,' Molly said. 'It's train number four. Maybe it's Dr Wiggott himself. He could be there waiting for you.'

Boy climbed over the locomotive of his train and into Minnie's carriage. He stepped onto the Waxworld and saw the street of old shops. Wax figures of shoppers stared into the windows then moved on to the next one. Street urchins chased one another around the gas street lamps that glowed a ghastly green-white light. Boy noticed that, as she ran around a large man in a fine top hat, a girl grabbed at him and screamed as if she were being chased by a monster.

'Desist, foolish child,' the man said, though he had a kindly face and didn't seem to mind too much. The girl ran off into an alley. Only Boy, the expert thief, noticed the flash of silver as she swept the man's stolen pocket watch into her ragged skirt pocket.

A man as small and sharp as William Hare

hid in the shadows and watched and smiled. He followed the girl into the alley to take the watch from his pickpocket child. He was her thief-master. He was the famous Ikey Solomon. 'What happened to Ikey Solomon in real life?' Boy asked Molly.

'In real life? He was transported to Australia and died miserably. In the Charles Dickens story *Oliver Twist* he was hanged,' Molly said. 'That's what they did to thieves like you.'

Boy blew out his cheeks. 'I'd better be careful then,' he said and stepped forward.

I never done nothing, not nothing at all

'There's an invisible beam in front of the Waxworld. When someone steps across it the scene comes to life,' Molly explained.

'I guessed that,' Boy said.

'I wonder who's been here before you,' Molly asked.

'If it was that plodding policeman or Loaf's one-eyed lout we'd see their wet footprints. We sent them into the sea. They can't have dried out yet.'

'Maybe there's someone in Wiggott's Wonderful Waxworld we don't know about,' Molly said. Then she cried, 'Look out!'

The brat-boy who'd been chasing the girl began to run around Boy. Fingers as fine as willow twigs brushed around Boy. He felt those fingers flutter, as light as moth wings, searching every pocket in his clothes. Anyone else would not have noticed. Boy did. He grabbed the ragamuffin by his skinny, dirt-crusted wrist. 'Pickpocket,' Boy hissed.

The child began to wail, 'Help, oh help! This big bully is hurting me. I never done nothing, not nothing at all.'

Ikey Solomon stepped from the shadows. 'What seems to be the trouble?' he asked in a whiny, wheedly voice.

'I caught this scruffy kid trying to rob me,' Boy said.

'Let me go, you're hurting me arm. I'm innocent as the day is long,' the child wailed. Shoppers turned and watched the drama. 'You can search me,' the child sniffed. 'I got nothing on me. If you find one penny in me pockets you won't need to hang me – I'll hang me-self. So help me I will.'

'I'll search him,' Ikey said and patted the boy's

soot-and-mud clothes with a thin, hard hand. 'Nothing rattling in there, sir,' he said to Boy.

A large man (who looked a lot like William Burke) stepped out of the alley. He carried a wooden stick too short and thick to be a walking stick. It was a club. A club heavy enough to knock out a horse[68]. He looked through his pig eyes at Boy and slapped the club in the palm of his left hand. 'You giving my lad bother?' he asked.

Ikey simpered, 'No, sir ... it's Mr Bill Sikes, isn't it, sir? No, Mr Sikes, a misunderstanding.' The thin thief-master looked at Boy. 'Isn't that right, young sir?'

Boy was breathing heavily and was working out how he could use the child as a shield, throw him at Sikes, snatch the club and take control. But Molly hissed, 'Say *yes* and let the child go.'

Boy lied through a tight jaw. 'I lost a pocket watch last week, so I suspect everyone who comes near me.'

Bill Sikes's piglet eyes gleamed. 'You have a pocket watch, do you?'

Boy glared at him. 'No. I *had* a pocket watch till some villain *stole* it.'

---

68 A really bad story-teller would call it a 'Pony Club'. But of course I'd never make such a feeble joke.

'So my little boy couldn't have been robbing you if you have nothing to rob,' Sikes said. 'I think you ought to say sorry to him.'

'Sorry,' Boy hissed. 'Sorry I didn't break your thieving, light-fingered, larcenous little arm,' he added.

Bill Sikes raised his club. At that moment Molly cried, 'Look out!'

I have some really good news for you

Boy turned his head in time to see a horse charging towards him. It was dragging a cart loaded with vegetables and the driver was struggling to stop it. 'Runaway horse!' Sikes cried and jumped aside.

Boy stared at it the way a rat stares at a cobra – unable to take his eyes off the death that was about to strike. As the horse's breath from its fiery nostril struck Boy in the face, he felt a firm push on his arm and was thrown onto the pavement. The mangling hooves sparked on the cobbles and the wheels crashed past as Boy gathered his breath.

He looked up slowly to see who had pushed him to safety. A lad about his own age grinned down at him. The round-faced lad looked a lot like Edwin the monk from Lindisfarne. Boy shook his head. 'Careless,' Molly murmured.

'You can't hang around on a London street,' the lad said[69].

'Thanks, Edwin,' Boy said quietly. 'I saved your life on Lindisfarne, now you've saved mine.'

The lad leaned close to Boy and asked, 'Did you get a blow to the head there? I'm not Edwin. . . I'm Charles. Charles Dickens.' He held out a hand to help Boy to his feet and Boy clung on and turned it into a handshake.

'Pleased to meet you, Charles.'

'And you are?'

Boy shook his head and remembered what Waxworld he was in and what Molly had told him. 'I'm Oliver. Oliver Twist.'

'What a great name,' Charles said. 'One day I may use that in a book.'

'You're a writer?' Boy asked.

Charles pulled a face. 'Not exactly. I work in

---

69 And you still can't. If the taxis don't get you, the buses will. But deadliest of all are the savage cyclists. Trust me, I'm a pedestrian.

a boot polish factory. But one day I want to be a writer.'

'I bet you'll do well,' Boy said.

'Look,' Charles said, 'you've had a shaking. Come to the tea room on the corner and sit down. I was just going there for my lunch.'

The two walked along the bustling street and entered the tea room. It had a bare wooden floor and slightly ragged lace tablecloths with tea stains, but the waitress was cheerful enough. She brought them a pot of tea and Boy supped it, grateful for a rest from the wild world of Wiggott's Wonderful Waxworld.

'My family's broke,' Charles sighed. 'Dad's in prison because he owes money. So I have to go out to work. But one day I'll write books. What about you? What do you do?'

Boy frowned as he tried to come up with a story that was partly the truth and partly the tale of Oliver Twist. 'I'm an orphan,' he began slowly. 'I have to do a few dishonest things to get by.'

Charles Dickens nodded, understanding. 'More exciting than my job in the factory . . . but more dangerous if you get caught.'

Boy nodded. 'I've been given a job. I have to take a telephone...'

'A what?'

'A ... a telegram ... to someone called Dr Wiggott. I just can't seem to find him. And I'm being chased by a policeman.'

'A what?'

'A constable.'

Charles Dickens grinned. 'I know what they are,' he said. 'Well, Oliver, I have some really good news for you.'

I have a terrible job

'I *need* some good news,' Boy said with a sigh. 'Then I can show you where Wiggott's Wonderful Wax Walkway is.'

Boy put his hands on the table and rose to his feet. He was still stiff from the fall. Charles waved him back down. 'We haven't had our tea yet. The Wiggott's Wonderful Wax Walkway isn't going anywhere. And you look like you need a rest.'

Boy sank back slowly. 'I do.'

Charles pulled a notebook from his pocket and a pen that he dipped into a bottle of ink. 'Tell me what it's like being a thief,' he said.

The thief asked, 'Are you going to report me to the police ... the constables?'

'Just tell him,' Molly said quietly.

Boy gave a sharp nod. 'I never tell anyone what I do. I don't share it,' he said, half to Molly, half to his new friend.

'So it's lonely,' Charles sympathised. 'I know what that means.'

'You have a family,' Boy said.

Charles sighed. 'Not really. I have a terrible job – I sit in a rat-infested London warehouse, just wrapping and tying and pasting labels onto jars of black boot polish. I walk five miles to get to work, and after ten hours I will walk that again to get back to my rented room. I only see my family on Sundays, when I go to the Marshalsea Prison. My father's in there for debt. My whole family has to live in that debtors' prison.'

'It sounds grim,' Boy said.

'But one thing that gets me through the night is my pen. I write down ideas for stories. No matter what happens – no matter how bad – I think I can make it into a story. That Ikey

Solomon you met outside ... he'd make a good story. And that bully Bill Sikes. And now you ... Oliver Twist.'

The waitress gathered the empty teapot along with a couple of cracked cups and a jug of milk with some dust and soot swimming in it[70]. 'That'll be a penny each,' she said.

Charles looked at Boy, his face as plain as a question mark. 'I don't have any money to spare,' he said. 'I thought you might.'

The waitress's face clouded like a summer storm. 'Ordering tea without the means to pay. That's a crime that is. I'm going to call the constable. He'll lock you both in Marshalsea.'

'Then I'll never get to Dr Wiggott,' Boy groaned.

A creaking voice behind Boy said, 'Don't worry... I'll pay.'

Boy swung round to see Ikey Solomon holding out two copper pennies in his grimy hand. 'Thank you, Mr Solomon,' Charles Dickens said. 'I'll pay you back some day.'

Ikey grinned a green-toothed grin. 'Oh, you can pay me back before the hour is out, my lad.

---

70 There's nothing wrong with soot in your tea, if you're a Georgian. Just think of it as soot-tea.

Wait two minutes then follow me out and see me on the corner. I have a little job you can help me with.'

How do we
stop the cart?

The boys left the tea room. Ikey Solomon pulled Boy into an alley between two shops. Young Charles Dickens followed. The alley was as dim and damp as Dank Alley outside Wiggott's back door. The rats were just as squeaky[71].

'Now, lads, Jack Dawkins is one of my dearest friends – a bit of an artful dodger, but a harmless lad – has been arrested for stealing pocket watches, silk handkerchiefs and purses. Of course he didn't do it, did young Jack. No, he was just looking after the things for a pal when

---

71 Some people say a thing is 'squeaky clean'. The rats in Dank Alley and in Ikey's London were squeaky dirty.

the constable stopped him and searched him. The judge didn't listen. No. He sentenced young Jack to hang.'

'When?' Boy said quietly.

'Noon today. They'll turn him off at Newgate.'

'Turn him off?' Boy asked.

'Send him up a ladder with a noose around his neck,' Charles explained, 'then turn the ladder so he drops.'

'Horrible,' Molly said quietly. 'Let's get out of here before they do it to you, Boy.'

But Ikey was going on: 'Of course, you can save the innocent lad. You and your friend here.'

'What? Ride in like a highwayman, cut the rope and carry him away from the gallows?' Charles asked.

Ikey looked at him with a pained face. 'That sort of thing only happens in storybooks. You should be a writer.'

'I'm going to be, one day,' Charles Dickens said.

The man's crooked eyebrows lifted in surprise. 'And are you going to put me in one of your books?' he asked.

The boy nodded. 'You *and* Oliver Twist here,' he said.

'Make sure you show me as a sort of Robin Hood ... stealing from the rich to give to the poor. You know the sort of thing,' the villain said and gave a wink.

'I'll make sure no one forgets your character,' Charles said.

'Wonderful. Now then, here's my plan to rescue poor Jack. You see, the cart that takes him to the gallows has to pass along this very road. All we have to do is stop it. Bill Sikes will jump on the cart, carry Jack off and take him to the blacksmith to have his chains cut off. That's all set up.'

'How do we stop the cart?' Boy asked.

Ikey leered like a vulture over a dying duck. 'That's the clever part of my plan,' he said. And he told Charles and Boy what they had to do.

You're a mumblecrust raggabrash

First there was a faint roar like waves on a distant seashore. Then Boy and Charles could ·hear it was the roar of human voices, cheering and jeering, mocking and heckling, catcalling and booing and hiss-whistling.

'There are always crowds that follow the cart to watch the executions,' Ikey explained. 'Get ready...'

The boys looked to the end of the street. A weary pair of horses dragged an open cart round the corner. The driver carried a whip to force the horses into a trot. A girl, a boy and two ragged men sat gloomily in the back of the cart; a guard with a musket sat beside them.

The crowd kept shouting so loud Boy almost missed Ikey's cry of, 'Go now!'

Boy ran into the middle of the road and shouted back, 'You're as ugly as a maggot.'

Charles Dickens marched after him and prodded him in the shoulder. 'Listen, you gobermouch with a dog's breath, you're a mumblecrust raggabrash.'

'Nice one,' Molly laughed. 'I wish I knew what it meant.' But she didn't have time to find out. Things were happening quickly now. Boy and Charles began to wrestle in the roadway, shouting and threatening to tear off ears, eyes, legs and noses.

The driver on the prison cart called, 'Get out of the road, you young dorbel skilamalinks.'

The boys stopped fighting and stood there looking at him. 'Saddle-goose and smellfungus,' Charles called to the man. The horses were about to trample the fighters when the carter stood up and hauled on the reins. Then he pulled on a handbrake so the wheels on the cart locked and skidded, slewed, swerved and stopped.

The prisoners and the guard were thrown to the floor. Before the guard could rise to his feet, Bill Sikes had climbed onto a wheel and leapt into the cart. He tore the musket away from the guard then tapped him on the skull with his thick stick. The man sank without a groan. Sikes snatched up Jack Dawkins, threw him over his shoulder and jumped down from the cart. The other prisoners heaved their chains and struggled onto the street and into the rat-run alleys.

The crowds cheered. They'd been cheated of a hanging today, but the escape was better than watching a play at the cheap theatres in Drury Lane. Boy and Charles grinned and shook hands. Ikey nodded and smiled from his shadow on the corner near the tripe dresser's shop[72].

The young Charles Dickens pointed to the end of the street. 'Wiggott's Wonderful Wax Walkway is at the end of the street. I have to run and see my family in Marshalsea,' he called and hurried away.

---

72 As you know, tripe is the stomach of a cow sold by a butcher as food. A 'tripe dresser' prepares the tripe for cooking – he scrubs out all the half-eaten grass. Loverly. He is NOT a shopkeeper who dresses people in tripe. Don't be so ridiculous, please.

Boy turned towards Wiggott's. 'At last,' he said.

'Not so fast,' a voice behind him said and a huge, hairy hand gripped his shoulder.

I saw what you did

It was a constable (who looked a lot like Constable Craig from the bodysnatching world of Burke and Hare – a world that was long gone[73].)

'I saw what you did,' the constable said.

'A harmless little fight in the street,' Boy said with a shrug of the one free shoulder. He wriggled under the talon that gripped his other shoulder.

'You helped a criminal to escape. The judge won't like that. In fact, the judge will probably send you to the gallows in place of the Dawkins lad. I'll take you to the court right now, but it's

---

73 You might almost say, 'Hare today and gone tomorrow.' You *might* say that . . . if you were clever and witty. Oh, never mind.

a waste of time,' the constable said with a sigh. 'May as well take you straight to the hanging. It's all set up ready.' He sighed again. 'But the law says you have to have a fair trial first. Come along now.'

Boy writhed and wriggled and wrought some more, but the constable had a little metal machine that he clamped to one of Boy's thumbs and then the other. It was just as good as handcuffs in keeping his hands trapped behind his back.

Boy looked at the alley for help from Ikey Solomon, but the thief-master had vanished like a morning mist in the noonday sun. As he was pushed along the street the crowds who had followed the hanging-cart stayed to laugh. He muttered into his pocket, 'So how do I get out of this one?'

After a while Molly replied, 'You don't. I said it was dangerous. This time you're really finished and there's nothing I can do.'

'Great,' Boy said in a voice as bitter as a winter wind. 'Great.'

The judge had a wig that was yellow with age and a face that was even yellower. He listened to the constable's report. 'Anything to say, boy ... what's your name, by the way?'

'Oliver Twist, sir,' Boy replied.

'Any reason why we shouldn't twist the rope round Twist's neck?' the judge said and his a sour-milk face gave a sour smile at his own joke.

'Hurr, hurr,' the constable laughed.

'I'm not guilty,' Boy cried.

'I don't believe you,' the judge said. He reached under his bench and pulled out a frayed square of black material and placed it on top of his wig. He raced through the sentence as if he'd said it a thousand times before ... which he had. 'Oliver Twist, you will be taken from here to the prison and from there to a place of execution, where you will be hanged by the neck until you are dead and then your body buried within the grounds of the prison, and may the Lord have mercy upon your soul.'

'It's not fair!' Boy wailed.

The judge looked sorrowful. 'Life's not fair, Twist. Life just isn't fair. Take him to Newgate, constable.'

Maybe I can pray
for a miracle

Boy was dragged away from the court to the prison next door. The constable rapped on the gloomy, doomy oak gates with his nightstick. 'Go away,' a voice said from the other side. 'We're full.'

'I have a prisoner for you,' the constable shouted back.

'Hard cheese. We're full. No room at the bin.'

'You have to take him,' the constable whined. 'It's only for a little while. They'll hang him as soon as they get the hangman out of the tavern.'

'There's other prisons, you know. Try the Marshalsea. They had spare rooms last I heard.'

'That's a prison for people that owe money,' the constable cried.

'So? A prison is a prison is a prison. As long as the villain's under lock and key, that's all that matters. A prison is a prison is a prison.'

'So you said,' the constable snapped angrily. He grabbed Boy roughly by the collar and marched him back through the miserable miles of the mud-guttered streets. At last, they arrived at a place that smelled even worse than the streets. Its greasy grey walls were guarded by greasy grey men under a greasy grey sky with greasy grey keys. You'll never guess what colour their socks were[74].

Boy choked on the smell of human filth and was pushed into a cell with a wooden plank for a bed and china pot for a toilet. The constable unfastened the thumb machine and said, 'I'll be back for you later.' The door was locked with a heavy crash-clank of a heavy key.

The only window in the room was high above Boy's head and was guarded with rusting iron

---

74 They were navy blue. I said you'd never guess.

bars. He sank onto the bed plank. 'So there really is no way out this time?' he said to Molly.

'Maybe I'll think of something,' she said kindly. 'I have a map of the Marshalsea prison here. 'There are drains under the floors ... if you can get to the prison kitchen and down a hatch.'

'Can I get to the kitchen?'

'Not unless you can get out of that door,' the girl-phone said.

'Any bright ideas about how I can open that door?' Boy snapped.

'No. Sorry,' Molly said.

'Maybe I can pray for a miracle,' Boy sighed.

He didn't hear the footsteps in the corridor or the harsh jangle of keys outside his door.

A far, far better thing I do now

Molly whirred as her memory searched for facts. She showed her fact page.

In 1825, there were forty-two hangings at Newgate. Not one of these was for murder. Twelve were for making forged banknotes, twelve for robbery or burglary and five for highway robbery.

'Thanks,' Boy said bitterly. 'I really wanted to know that.' Molly read on. . .

> On the eve of a hanging, the gallows were brought out by a team of horses and placed in front of Newgate Prison. Large crowds gathered around it and it was guarded by soldiers with pikes. Wealthy people could pay as much as ten pounds for a seat in a window overlooking the gallows at the hanging of a really famous criminal.

'Shut up,' Boy said and shook the phone in his hand.

'But I am going through a list of all the names,' she said, patient as a statue standing under a pigeon.

'Good for you,' Boy snarled.

'Your name isn't there ... no one named Oliver Twist was executed.'

Boy sighed. 'That was in London in 1825. This is in Wiggott's Wonderful Waxworld now. It's different here. Soon that door will open and...'

The door opened.

A guard stood there. His face would have been

pale if you washed off the dirt. A lad pushed past him wearing a bright red cap and scarf. 'Hello, Oliver,' he said with a grin.

The guard swung the door shut with a clang and the rattling keys locked it behind the lad. He pulled off the red cap. Boy blinked. 'Charles? Charles Dickens?'

Charles gave a deep bow. 'Your servant, sir.'

'Have you come to watch me hang?' Boy asked, in a grapefruit-sour voice.

Charles shrugged. 'I came to help you escape,' he said simply. 'I was in here visiting my family when I saw you brought in. I have a plan so daring I might use it one day when I'm a writer.'

'What is it?' Boy grunted, not believing.

'The guard saw a boy walk in here with a red cap and scarf. He will see a boy walk out with a red cap and scarf[75]. The boy who walked in was me. The boy who walks out will be you.'

'It won't work,' the young thief said.

'It does,' Molly said. 'In Charles's book *A Tale of Two Cities*. Of course, the man that entered the prison was executed while the prisoner escaped.'

Boy repeated that to Charles. 'They could

75 A trick that would only work if the guard was stupid. But was he? Wait and see.

execute you in my place.'

Charles shrugged again. 'It's Oliver Twist that was sentenced to hang. When they find they have the wrong boy, they'll have to let me go.'

'It's such a risk,' Boy said. 'So brave.'

Molly agreed. 'It is a far, far better thing you do now than you have ever done before,' she said.

'A far, far better thing I do now than I have ever done before?... Hey, I could use that line in my book. Now put on my hat and scarf and call the guard to let you out.'

Which is just what Boy did.

Is the tripe terrible?

Meanwhile ... in another Waxworld ... let us not forget Igon, Arfur Loaf's evil assistant, and PC L.O. Elloe, Wildpool's newest policeman[76].

They had stepped through Blackbeard's cabin door and into the icy waters of the North Sea. When they climbed back out they were cold and shivering. The damp Dank Alley air was not going to dry them quickly. They reversed the train all the way back to Billy Crudge's platform.

'Take your trousers off,' the old caretaker said.

---

76 What do you mean you HAD forgotten them? This slightly terrifying twosome on the trail of terror must never be forgotten. The same as you should never forget to brush your teeth twice a day.

'My mum wouldn't like that,' PC Elloe gasped.

'Your mum wouldn't like you catching a cold. I have a heater in my room,' Billy boasted. 'They'll be dry in no time. You can set off to catch your criminal in comfort.'

It took a while for the clothes to dry ... long enough for Boy to be arrested, thrown in jail and escape.

'So where do we find the thieving boy ... and the phone?' Igon asked.

The caretaker looked at the map on the wall. A green light glowed as still as starlight on a frosty night. 'They've stopped at the Waxworld of Ikey Solomon in the Chamber of Terrors. The most dangerous place in all of Wiggott's Waxworld,' the caretaker explained.

'Ooooh, the Chamber of Terrors. Even more terrible than wet trousers?' PC Elloe asked as he slipped his warm, dry ones back on.

Billy Crudge leaned forward. 'Listen, I can tell you, officer, that this is the Waxworld where they may find Wiggott's office ... if they survive the grim gallows and the putrid prisons, the cruel constables and the terrible tripe.'

'Is the tripe terrible?' Igon asked.

'Only if you eat it,' Billy Crudge said. 'It's fine to wear in on your head or use it as a tea cosy. But I wouldn't eat it myself.'

'I won't,' the policeman said with a shudder.

'Get back on the train and boldly go to that final frontier,' Billy said, 'with a mission to explore a strange new world, to seek out new life and new civilization and to boldly go where no man has gone before. But be warned, you are in for a bit of a trek.'

'I could be a star ... on my first day at work,' PC Elloe said ... boldly.

'And I could get to keep my job,' Igon said with a nod. 'Come on, constable, let's boldly go where no bold man has gone be-boldly-fore.'

'Once I put my trousers on,' PC Elloe said. 'Ooooh, they're lovely and warm.'

And so they went. Boldly.

I'm thrilled to fluffy mint balls

The guard let Boy out of the prison cell[77].
Even the horse-dung, stagnant-mud-gutter
smell of the street smelled fresh after the prison
air. Molly found a London map of 1825 and guided
Boy back to the street where they'd started. 'We
entered just in front of the tea room,' Molly
reminded Boy. 'You can get back to the Waxworld
that way ... or you can go to the end of the street
and try to find Wiggott himself in that place he
calls the Wax Walkway.'

Boy chewed on a lip. 'We've come this far,'
he said. 'I may as well hand over the phone to

---

77 Yes, he really was that stupid. Some of us are.

Wiggott and get the payment.'

'Then you can finally go back into the real world and rescue me from Loaf Tower,' Molly said.

'Yes,' Boy said. 'I'll find a way.'

Ikey Solomon and Bill Sikes were nowhere to be seen – not even in the shadow of the shadows in the alley. But the crowds were still on the streets, even though there was no hanging to watch. They were heading towards the end of the row of shops. There stood a rambling, shambling, mangled and tangled building with a candled, gold-spangled sign saying:

WIGGOTT'S WONDERFUL WAX WALKWAY

See wax figures of the famous
So real you can almost hear them breathe
One penny per person

'I don't have a penny,' Boy said to Molly.

'A penny? You don't need a penny,' said a

creaky voice from behind a window set in the wall by the door. Underneath the window the words *Box Office* had been painted in gold.

'You'll let me in free,' Boy said. 'Why?'

A very old woman peered through the glass at him. 'Because you are looking for Dr Wiggott and I want you to find him.'

'Why?' he repeated.

'Y? Y? Y?' the woman parroted. 'Don't you know any other letters of the alphabet? Like the letter Q. A quaint and quirky letter. Or R? A red letter day if you get that.'

Boy was bewildered. 'Are you mad?'

'No. Are you?'

'How do you know I need to see Dr Wiggott and why would you help me?'

'That's two questions. Which do you want me to answer first?' the woman squawked.

'The second,' Molly said.

'I want to help you because I am a member of the famous threesome ... the Ladies Who Crunch. We've been watching Loaf Tower and we reckon Molly Maltby, the missing girl, is in there.'

'You're right,' Boy said.

'Clever-clogged Edna said so. We're too old to rescue her. But you could do it, lad. As for *how* we know you want to see Dr Wiggott ... well, you told the daft old caretaker when you came in here.'

'Ah,' Boy nodded. 'So where will I find Wiggott?'

'I don't know,' the woman said. 'Hang on a minute.' She vanished from the box office window and appeared through a small door at the side. 'My name is Minnie Cooper. I've been following you ... then waiting for you. I've got a job here, collecting the pennies. But I don't know what's behind those swinging doors. Maybe we can explore together?'

'Thank you, Miss Cooper,' Molly said politely.

'I'm thrilled to fluffy mint balls to think I can help to rescue you, lass. Lead on, Boy, to death or glory.' They stepped through the red, swinging doors that swung shut behind them.

I thought I'd find you here

V isitors' voices murmured and made the Wax
Walkway sound like a beehive of busyness.
People walked around looking at wax figures of
fame or fun.

A man in a cap looked at a model and lifted
the cap to scratch his head. 'Who's that geezer,
Gertrude?' he asked the skin-thin woman beside
him.

She bent to read the label. 'It says it's William
Shakespeare,' she told him.

'What did he do? He's not shaking no spear.
He's got a feather in his hand. What's that about?

Is he a famous murderer what tickled people to death? Hurr, hurr.'

'Alfred, stop showing me up,' she snapped snippily. 'Let's get to the front before the grand opening.'

They shuffled and elbowed their way towards a figure that was covered with a large red cloth. A mystery figure. A young lady in a fine, green silk dress walked up and down in front of the covered figure. She chewed on her white glove, patted her hat, chewed her glove, and wound a ringlet of hair around her finger.

Someone tapped Boy on the shoulder. It was Charles Dickens. 'Hello, Oliver,' he said brightly. 'I thought I'd find you here. Met Dr Wiggott yet?'

Boy shook his head. 'They let you out?'

Charles nodded. 'I told you they would. I really will use that dodge in one of my books one day. But first I have to finish *your* book – well, I'm just writing it in my head at the moment. Ikey Solomon will be the villain – though I'll call him Fagin – along with Bill Sikes. I need a wife for Bill Sikes. What do you think I should call her?'

Before Boy could reply a gaslight above the

figure flared brighter, a curtain at the back was pulled aside and a man stepped through. Boy blinked hard and croaked, 'Mr Crudge the caretaker? What's he doing here?'

The old man clapped his hands and the buzz of the crowd fell silent. 'Welcome to Wiggott's Wax Walkway for the launch of a new figure.'

'Where's Dr Wiggott?' Boy cried.

Billy Crudge glared at Boy. 'He never meets the public. He is a shy and secret man. He leaves all this stuff to me. Now shut up and let me get on with the opening.'

Boy was about to moan that he *had* to see Wiggott – that he's faced deadly dangers for the chance to see him – but Billy Crudge was resting his hand on a white cloth that covered a waxwork figure and shouting to the gathering crowds, 'Here he is ... one of the greatest inventors ever to walk the Earth. His name, you will guess, is Jacques Montgolfier.'

'Ooooh,' the crowd gasped.

Boy just said, 'Who?[78]'

Molly flickered and showed him.

---

78 And you are probably asking the same thing. Jacques who? Villains like Julius Caesar or Henry VIII are remembered for their very badness. Some great and good people, like Montgolfier, are just forgotten. Sad.

> Jacques Montgolfier was one of the first men to fly. He and his brother built a hot-air balloon. In 1783 they sent a sheep, a duck and a rooster into the sky. Two months later two humans flew over Paris. The Montgolfier brothers became the most famous men in the world.

Billy Crudge the caretaker was speaking again. 'And today, to uncover his model, we are thrilled and happy and pleased as Punch to have his granddaughter, Nancy.'

'That's it,' Charles Dickens muttered. 'I'll call Bill Sikes's wife ... Nancy.'

'Shhhh,' the people around him hissed as the lady in the fine green dress and white gloves, Nancy Montgolfier, stepped forward. She uncovered the model of her grandfather, gave a sweet speech (with a French accent) about her grandfather and then said there was an even greater thrill for visitors. Billy Crudge helped her pull open the curtains at the back. And there it stood, huge and colourful, awesome and amazing.

The crowd gasped.

They'll make you chief constable by next week

PC Elloe and the eyepatched Igon stepped off the train again. They looked around the street. This was the dangerous time. The time when they couldn't *see* any danger ... but they knew it must be there, because this was Wiggott's Wonderful Waxworld's Chamber of Terror.

Groups of prattling people were drifting down the street like snow. Except they weren't white. And they weren't cold. And they wouldn't melt into puddles of water if you stood them in front of a fire. Apart from *that*, they were like snow.

'Where are you all going?' Laurence Olivier

Elloe asked a lady in a black dress carrying a black brolly. The woman narrowed her eyes. She looked at Igon as if he were some sort of evil assistant to an evil inventor. She just pointed to a large red and gold poster on the wall by the galloon salesman's shop[79].

The poster read:

WIGGOTT'S WAX WALKWAY

PRESENTS

AN AMAZINGLY AWESOME NEW ATTRACTION

NOT ONLY A NEW FAMOUS FIGURE

BUT

A BEHEMOTH, A LEVIATHAN, A JUGGERNAUT –
A TOWERING, TITANICALLY HUGE PIECE OF HISTORY

WHAT IS IT? A MYSTERY.

NEVER BEFORE SEEN IN ENGLAND

THE BEST PENNY YOU'LL EVER SPEND

Opens at 3:00 p.m. on Monday

---

79 That is a lie. The poster was on the wall by the die-sinker's shop. I just like the word *galloon* and wanted to use it again. Galloon, galloon, galloon. There, that's better.

'What is it?' PC Elloe asked.

'If we knew *that* it wouldn't be a mystery,' Igon pointed out. 'But if it's one of Wiggott's wonders – a Wax Walkway within his Wonderful Waxworld – I guess that's where we'll find the boy-thief.'

The policeman's face was as bright as his new buttons. 'Then I can arrest a master-criminal on my first day at work.'

'Hmmmm,' Igon snorted. 'At that rate they'll make you chief constable by next week.'

Elloe glowed. 'Chief constable? The job of Mr Betterton Nunn himself? The Bald Eagle, the constables call him. Of course, I would never be so cheeky as to call our leader by a nickname. Do you really think I could get Mr Nunn's job?'

'No,' the eyepatched man snapped. 'Let's go inside and see what all the fuss is about.'

They walked past the empty box office without paying a penny and entered the Wax Walkway just as Billy Crudge the caretaker was pulling back the curtains. The audience gasped.

'A behemoth,' they cried. 'A leviathan, a juggernaut – a towering, titanically huge piece of history.' And so it was.

It's not what
I expected

When the long red curtains parted, the visitors saw a large basket, large enough to carry six people ... or a sheep, a duck and a rooster. It was draped with red and blue cloth and decorated with eagles.

Then the amazed audience looked upwards towards the ceiling. The floor above had been cut away to let a massive balloon rise to the roof. It was deep blue like an evening sky and covered with pictures of star signs, suns and the face of the French King, Louis XVI[80].

They gasped. Even Boy was amazed. 'It's not what I expected,' he said.

'It's not what I expected,' Charles Dickens said.

'And you had great expectations,' Molly chuckled.

'*Great Expectations*? What a great title for a book,' Charles said and scribbled it on his notepad.

At that moment PC L.O. Elloe placed a hand on Boy's shoulder. 'I would like you to accompany me to the station,' he said.

'I don't want to catch a train,' Boy said with a smile.

'I meant the *police* station. I am arresting you for the theft of a mobile phone thingy from Loaf Tower.'

The crowds of visitors saw trouble with a constable and melted away like snow ... except

---

80 If you stayed awake in your history lessons, you would know that King Louis XVI was the French king who had his head cut off on a guillotine ten years after the famous balloon was built. The picture showed him when his head was still attached to his body. His head flew ... ten years later his head flew off.

they weren't cold or white or . . . you know the rest.

Boy pointed at Igon. 'He's the one you should be arresting. He's part of the plot to kidnap Molly Maltby. Arrest him, solve the kidnap and they'll make you chief constable within a week.'

Igon's eye blinked like a hummingbird's wing. 'No. No. I never agreed with that kidnapping. I told Mr Loaf it was a wicked thing to do – that he should experiment on his own brain. Spare me. I can't go to prison.' A tear trickled down from his eye.

Minnie Cooper stepped forward. 'You're a wicked little man,' she said. 'If you really feel sorry for Molly you'll help me to rescue her from your evil master-minded master.'

'I would if I could,' Igon wept. 'But since that boy stole the phone Molly is even more carefully guarded than before. I won't get into Loaf Tower without the phone . . . and it's for sure no one else will.'

'Every fortress has a weakness,' Charles Dickens said.

Igon shook his head. 'Every door is guarded and locked. There's only one secret way in . . .

and that's impossible.'

The soft French voice of Nancy Montgolfier said, 'I remember Louis XVI's wife asked her minister to get a large sum of money. He said, "Madame, if it is possible it has been done; if it is impossible it SHALL be done." The impossible, it is nothing to the Montgolfiers. What is this secret way in?' she asked.

'There is a door in the roof of Loaf Tower,' Igon said. 'But we can't climb a sheer glass tower. And we can't fly.'

Nancy smiled gently. She turned and looked at the huge balloon. 'Oh yes we can,' she said. *'Oh yes we can.'*

What is that talking thing?

'A balloon?' Boy laughed. 'We can't fly a balloon.'

'Why not? My grandfather did,' Nancy said. 'This is the very balloon he flew fifty kilometres. How far is this Loaf Tower?'

'A few hundred metres and a couple of hundred years away,' Molly said. 'But we could do it. If Dr Wiggott would let us break through the roof.'

'He will,' Billy Crudge the caretaker said. 'He will.'

Boy was an expert at breaking in and breaking out. With a long pair of Mr Crudge's ladders he climbed to the roof of Wiggott's Wonderful Waxworld and began to push the slates out. They showered down onto Dank Alley below and scattered rats every way. Inside the building a hundred years of dust floated down and froze the rays of the sun.

The afternoon sunlight struck the blue balloon and it glowed like the fire Nancy was building in the fire-basket below. Billy Crudge offered them chairs and tables from Dr Wiggott's office to throw on once the balloon was free.

'How do we steer?' Minnie Cooper asked.

'The wind is west-by-south-west, so it's almost right to carry you from here to Loaf Tower,' Molly said, checking the weather station news.

'What is that talking thing?' Charles Dickens asked as he sawed at a table leg and sweated.

'It's magic,' Boy called down from the roof. There was no point trying to explain a phone to a lad from 1825 who hadn't even seen anything electric.

'You can rock the basket a little and it can steer the balloon a little,' Nancy explained. 'I'll come with you and show you,' she offered.

'No,' Mr Crudge said sharply. 'You're part of Dr Wiggott's Waxworld. Once you leave you'll run out of charge.'

'Charge? I do not know what your English word means,' Nancy said.

The caretaker simply said, 'You must stay here, Miss Montgolfier. And you, Young Master Dickens... It's one of the ways of Wiggott's Waxworld.'

Charles Dickens shrugged. 'I'll stay ... so long as I don't suffer hard times.' He carried on helping to find the wood to fuel the great balloon.

As the softly choking smoke rose from the fire-basket over their heads, Minnie Cooper talked eagerly to Nancy to learn what the ropes and levers did. PC Elloe and Igon the evil assistant helped load broken tables and chairs – the fuel. They climbed into the passenger basket.

The hole in the Waxworld roof was large enough now. The balloon tugged at its ropes, straining to leap upwards. Boy climbed back down the ladder and joined Minnie in the basket. She pushed at some bellows so the fire glowed, the hot air rose and the balloon ropes creaked.

'Goodbye, Charles Dickens ... one day I'll read your books.'

'Do you think I'll become a writer?' the lad asked, a little shy and unsure now.

'Oh, I know you will,' Boy grinned[81]. 'Goodbye, Nancy. Untie us, Mr Crudge.'

'No,' Billy Crudge said and he licked his wrinkled lips greedily. 'First you give me that phone. *You* can go ... rescue the girl if you like ... but the phone stays.'

81 It is so easy to see into the future when you've travelled back in time. You try it some time and see.

He's too daft to see the dangers ahead

B oy threw his head back and laughed[82]. 'I hand the phone over when Dr Wiggott hands over the thousand pound reward.'

Billy Crudge gave a small nod. He reached into the pocket of his dull, brown overall and pulled out a wadge of ten pound notes bound in a paper band. 'One thousand pounds,' he said.

Boy's mouth went dry. It was what he wanted. It was what he didn't want. The policeman looked stern. A thief was selling stolen property under his very nose.

---

82 When I say he 'threw his head back' I really mean he threw it *backwards*. He didn't step into the basket then throw his head back into Wiggott's Wax Walkway. Don't try that at home ... you'll make a right mess on the carpet.

Igon's eye glittered. The precious phone was going to be sold under *his* very nose. The phone he'd spent so long creating.

Minnie gave a wrinkled little smile.

Charles Dickens and Nancy Montgolfier didn't understand what was happening ... but they felt the sunbeamed air was as tense as the rope holding the great blue balloon.

Boy looked at the face of the girl on the phone. Her smile was as strange as Minnie Cooper's. 'What do you think, Molly?' he asked her.

'I'm not Molly,' she said. 'Molly is tied to a table somewhere in Loaf Tower. You're just looking at a machine.'

'A really brilliant machine,' Igon objected.

'You can always build another,' the phone told him. 'But if Molly dies you can never replace her. Never.'

'But you've helped me so much,' Boy moaned. 'You rescued me time and again. Now you could help me rescue you... I mean rescue Molly.'

'You need brains, courage, cunning and knowledge,' the phone told him. 'Igon has the knowledge – he knows the way the building and the people there work. PC Elloe has the courage.'

'Thank you,' the young constable said seriously.

'He's too daft to see the dangers ahead, so he'll plunge in where sensible people hold back.'

'Oh,' L.O. Elloe sighed. 'Thank you.'

'And as for brains, you have one of the most wonderful wits of Wildpool in that balloon basket.'

'Thanks,' Boy said.

Now it was the phone's turn to laugh. 'I meant Minnie Cooper,' she said.

'Thanks,' Boy grumbled. 'I suppose that leaves me to be the cunning one?'

'There's nobody better in Wildpool,' the phone said gently. 'Maybe not in the whole world. Hand over the phone, take the money, then go and be a greater hero than any of the figures in Wiggott's Wonderful Waxworld.'

And Boy handed over the phone to Billy Crudge the caretaker.

Nancy sighed, Charles clapped softly, Igon groaned, PC Elloe tutted and Minnie grinned.

Billy Crudge passed the money to Boy, then he loosened the rope that held the flying machine.

She's playing with paper planes now

What would you do or say if a big, blue balloon flew over your town? If it carried a thief, an evil assistant, an old lady and a policeman? You would look up in wonder and say, 'Goodness me ... look at that amazing balloon. I wonder what those people are doing up there.'

Or you may say, 'Goodness me, that's dangerous. At least, it will be dangerous if it lands on my head.'

Or you may say, 'What a fine replica of the Montgolfier Balloon as flown over Paris on 19 September 1783[83].'

---

83 But if you said that, you are probably some sad history teacher with a head stuffed full of boring facts. You need to forget the facts and see the beauty of balloons.

What did the people of Wildpool do or say?
Nothing.

'What? Nothing at all?' you gasp. 'Why not?'
you gasp.

Because, I gasp back, the people of Wildpool
were a dull crowd under a cloud of grey each day.
They looked down in the gutter and not up at
the stars. They were a miserable people with a
lot to be miserable about.

Only two old ladies looked up. They were two-
thirds of the Ladies Who Crunch. They sat at a
table outside a café opposite Loaf Tower all day
and made their bitter coffee last for hours. They
looked up at Loaf Tower and wondered what
went on behind the great pyramid of smoked-
glass windows.

The other third of the Ladies Who Crunch
was in the balloon looking down. 'Yoo-hoo,'
Minnie called. Now you may think this was
foolish. A secret team of rescuers tries to be as,
well, *secret* as possible. And shouting, 'Yoo-hoo,'
gives the game away.

But Minnie Cooper was a wise woman. Edna
squinted up and turned to Marjorie Door.

'I see Minnie's up to her madcap tricks again. We sent her off to find a thief and rescue a kidnapped girl. And what does she do?' Mrs Crudge complained. 'What does she do? She goes joy-riding in a balloon. She'll feel the sharp edge of my tongue when she gets back down here.'

'Maybe,' Marjorie Door said quietly as she knitted on. 'Maybe that's part of her plan. We should wait and see.'

'Pah,' Edna Crudge said sourly. The truth is she knew her friend Marjorie was right. 'I'm still keeping a sharp edge on my tongue, Marjorie. If I don't use it on Minnie, I can use it on Billy when I get home.'

As they stared up at the drifting balloon a white triangle appeared and drifted down. 'A paper aeroplane,' Marjorie said.

'I can see that,' Edna raged. 'She's not satisfied with gallivanting in a balloon ... which I can tell you is a replica of the Montgolfier Balloon as flown over Paris on 19 September 1783 ... she's playing with paper planes now.'

The plane came down on a corkscrew path

and landed at Marjorie Door's feet. She looked down and gasped.

'Minnie isn't playing,' she whispered. 'She's sending us a secret message. Look, it says on the paper wing . . . *Secret Message.*'

'So unfold it,' Edna snapped.

'I can't,' her crunching comrade cried.

'Why not?'

'Cos it's secret.'

It's a task for
someone with brains

E dna's crab-claw fingers nipped the paper
plane from Marjorie's trembling hand and
unfolded it. The message read:

Dear Edna and Marjorie,
The girl is a prisoner in Loaf Tower and
I am on my way to rescue her. I wonder
if you could come up with a plan to get
Mr Arfur Loaf away from the tower while we
carry out the rescue.
Yours faithfully,
Minnie Cooper (Miss)

Marjorie clacked her knitting needles. The scarf she was knitting would have fitted a giraffe ... or a diplodocus[84]. 'Are you going to tell me what's in that secret message?' Marjorie said with a sniff. Marjorie was sounding a bit huffy and we can't blame her. Ooooh, that Edna was such a bossy boots she would make a saint snap or a mild-mannered monk moan.

'We have to lure Arfur Loaf out of his tower while Minnie and her friends break into it. It's a task for someone with brains,' Edna said and scratched her grey-haired head through her purple pom-pommed hat.

Marjorie clacked on and (if you looked through a magnifying glass) you could just see a tiny smile at the corners of her mouth.

Edna went on, 'We could knock on the door and tell him his tower is on fire ... but that wouldn't work. They must have fire alarms. Or we could say there are rats in the sewers under Loaf Tower and it's about to collapse.' She scratched till the purple bobble was frayed. 'No, he wouldn't

84 In fact, if the diplodocuses had all had Marjorie's scarfs they wouldn't have died of cold and become extinct. Their eggs would have hatched and not been egg-stinct. But Marjorie wasn't around in Jurassic times ... and a diplodocus was too clumsy to knit. They got cold necks ... or were chewed by Tyrannosaurus Nex.

believe we are from Wildpool Council Drains Department. Ohhhh,' she sighed. 'I wish I had Minnie's brains.'

Marjorie knitted faster and said, 'Of course, you could just tell him your husband Billy Crudge has Arfur's precious phone at Wiggott's Wonderful Waxworld. That would get him running down Dank Alley.'

'Pah,' Edna sneered. 'That would never work because . . . because . . . well . . . it might just work,' Edna said. 'I'll tell you what I've decided. I will go to Loaf Tower and tell Arfur Loaf that my Billy has his precious phone. Hah,' she snorted. 'Who needs Minnie Cooper's brain when I have so many brilliant ideas myself? Eh, Marjorie? I say who needs her?'

'You're right, Edna. It's a brilliant idea. Off we go.'

Marjorie clacked her last and cast off her scarf. Some giraffe with a sore throat would be thrilled to see it. Two Ladies Who Crunch set off for the terrible tower across the road.

I'm afraid
of heights

The balloon was smoky and choky for the
rescue team in the basket below. But they
braved the stinging clouds and drifted across
towards the tall tower.

Minnie was as skilled at steering as Christopher
Columbus ... no, she was *better* than Columbus.
He just set off to the west and hoped to hit some
land. Minnie was aiming for a small circle on top
of Loaf Tower with the letter H in the middle...
H for 'Helipad'.

If you or I had been steering the Montgolfier
marvel it would have been H for 'Hopeless',

'Helpless', 'Hapless', 'Ha ha, you missed'. But Minnie guided it down to land feather-soft on the H. Igon jumped down and tied a rope from the balloon to one of the railings around the roof – railings put there to stop careless people falling off and making a mess like strawberry jam on the ground below.

PC Elloe followed and helped Minnie Cooper down. Boy was last. He made sure there was enough dry wood left to start a fresh fire. He remembered his lessons well – never go into a place till you are sure you have a safe way out.

There was a small door in a cabin at the corner of the roof, a cabin well out of the way of helicopter blades. It led to a stairway down into Loaf Tower. PC Elloe walked across and tried the handle. 'Locked,' he said. 'We'll have to find another way in.'

'Either that or break down the door,' Igon said.

'Too noisy,' Boy argued. 'Loaf's louts would hear it, run upstairs and throw us off the roof.'

'They wouldn't dare,' PC Elloe croaked. 'They can't throw me off. I'm afraid of heights.'

'Once you hit the pavement you'd be cured

of that forever,' Boy muttered. 'Let me try to unfasten the lock.'

He bent over and fiddled with a skeleton key for a few minutes, sweat starting to run into his eyes[85]. He looked at the waiting rescue team. 'It's no use. I've never seen a lock like this before,' he sighed. Minnie Cooper stepped forward and peered through her glasses at the problem.

'It's a Falcon 365 double-tumbler half-ratchet imperial lock from 1936. Clever Mr Loaf knows young thieves today won't be trained to unlock it.'

'I'm not,' Boy said.

'I am,' Minnie replied. She pulled a hair grip from her hair and bent it with fingers faster than Marjorie Door's nimble knitters. Boy watched and learned as Minnie explained the way the lock worked and its weakness. In half a minute it clicked open. 'There we are,' Minnie said. She was satisfied, but not boastfully proud.

'In we go,' PC Elloe said.

'No,' Minnie told him. 'Let's wait till Arfur Loaf is out of the way. She walked across to the railings round the roof and looked down to the street far below.

---

85 And here's a top tip: if you ever want to break into a graveyard, use a skeleton key.

'Ooooh, I feel giddy,' the policeman said, swooning and swaying. 'It's a long way down.'

Minnie sighed. She watched as two Ladies Who Crunch crossed the road and rang the buzzer on the great glass doors of Loaf Tower.

Waiting for a frog to kiss her

Arfur Loaf's evil eyes looked at the sleeping body of Molly Maltby. The room was dim, lit only with hidden lights that gave off a grim green glow like swamp gas.

The woman in the scarlet suit scowled and looked at her watch. 'It's been hours now and you haven't found that phone,' she said. 'I am not handing over the ten million pounds until I have it in my hands, working.'

Arfur Loaf, who was starting to look a lot like William Burke, twisted his hands together. 'Oh, Lady Greystoke...' he wittered in his squeaky voice.

'Grey-*stone*,' she said angrily.[86]

'Lady Grey-*stone*,' Loaf said. 'The phone is nothing. Igon can make me another. It's the way I wire up the brain to power a phone that's so clever. That's what makes it worth ten million.'

The woman glared at the evil inventor. 'Mr Oaf...'

'Loaf,' he whined, his mouth almost dribbling with greed as he thought of the ten million waiting for him.

'Mr Loafer... I am *not* going to have a girl sleeping in the cellar in Greystone Castle like Sleeping Beauty waiting for a frog to kiss her.'

'It was a prince that kissed Sleeping Beauty,' Arfur said with a light laugh. 'The frog-prince is a different fairy tale altogeth—'

'Mr Loathe, I am not interested in fairy stories. I am interested in having the most powerful little computer in the world. With that phone I can make ten *billion* pounds. But I do not ... hear me?... I do NOT want a sleeping girl in my basement.'

Arfur Loaf threw his hands in the air. 'But

---

86 It's an easy mistake to make. Lord Greystoke was the real name of the ape-man known as Tarzan. Lady Greystone was tired of being mistaken for the wife of a man in leopard-skin knickers with a cheetah for a best friend. You would be, too.

Lady Greystoke ... -stone... Stray-stone, that is the clever part of my plan. You will *not* have a sleeping girl. You will simply have her brain. I plan to remove her brain, keep it alive in a special fluid I have invented and wire it up to transmit its thoughts.'

The woman in scarlet frowned. 'But what about her body?'

Loaf shrugged. 'We won't need that.'

'What will you do with it?'

'Probably dump it in Wildpool canal in a bag with a few bricks to make it sink. No one will ever find it.'

Her ladyship leaned forward and showed her sharp teeth. 'You have kidnapped this girl,' she hissed. 'Now you are planning to murder her?'

'If her brain is still alive ... in a box ... it's not really murder, is it?' he smiled.

'Maybe the police will not see it that way.'

'Our millions of pounds will silence the police, Lady Straybone,' Loaf said in a voice soft as a dove.

'And if it doesn't work?' the woman asked, her diamonds glittering as hard as her voice.

'Then we try again with another brain. There's a very clever lad – he stole the phone. Once Igon has captured him we could try again with *his* brain.'

The lady in scarlet – whose name was not Straybone – said, 'Show me how you plan to remove the brain.'

Arfur Loaf reached into a shining metal toolbox and took out a small electric saw.

Please, sir, it's urgent, sir

A rfur Loaf turned a switch and the round blade on the saw spun round, whisper quiet with jackal-hungry teeth looking for some bone to bite into.

He brushed strands of the girl's hair off her forehead, licked his lips and lowered the saw.

There was a timid knock at the door. 'Go away,' he shouted.

'Please, sir, it's urgent, sir,' the timid knocker said . . . timidly.

'It can wait half an hour while I cut the top off a skull and place the brain in brine.'

'It's about Igon and the phone, sir,' the knocker said. It was a woman with a voice as trembling as a flute.

'Half an hour,' Loaf said and lowered the saw again.

'No,' Lady Greystone barked. 'It will take time to make a new phone. If we get the stolen phone back we can test it today with the brain in a box. You could even have your ten million pounds today.'

Loaf clicked the switch and the whispering saw whispered into silence. 'Enter,' Loaf ordered.

The humble assistant opened the door looking as sheepish as a flock of sheep caught on a ram raid[87]. 'Give me the phone, humble assistant,' the lady in red demanded.

'I don't have the phone,' the humble woman said. 'But there's someone here who knows where it is.'

Loaf turned brick-red with rage. 'No one sees inside the secrets of Loaf Tower,' he raged.

'Except me,' Lady Greystone said.

'Except Lady Payphone,' Loaf agreed.

'And the staff,' the humble servant said.

---

87 Ewe know what I mean.

'And the staff.'

'And the boy that stole the phone.'

'Yes, yes, yes,' Loaf sighed. 'But apart from Lady Maypole and the staff and the boy that stole the phone, NO one enters these secret walls.'

'And you,' Lady Greystone said.

Arfur Loaf looked weary enough to die on the spot. 'Who is it?' he said.

Edna Crudge and Marjorie Door, with her knitting, pushed past the humble servant. 'It is we . . . the Ladies Who Crunch,' Edna said grandly.

'And we bring news from Wiggott's Wonderful Waxworld,' Marjorie Door added.

'What news?'

'Go to the Waxworld at once and Igon will give you the phone you seek,' Marjorie said, getting as grand as Edna.

'Why can't he bring it to me himself?' Loaf asked.

'Good question,' Edna said.

'And do you have a good answer?' the lady in red asked red-faced . . . even though her name was grey . . . sort of.

'Because...' Edna began. 'Because...'

'Because wicked Wiggott has put Igon's eyepatch over his good eye and he can't see to find the way back,' Marjorie cried.

'The villain,' Arfur Loaf cried. 'I'm on my way.'

Edna smiled. 'Oh good. We'll look after your tower for you.'

Loaf left with the lady. The coast was clear as a newly washed window.

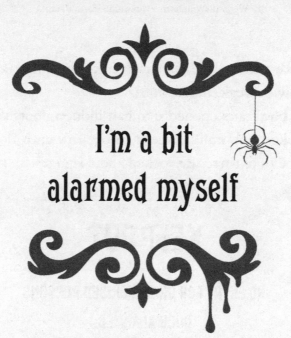

I'm a bit alarmed myself

L oaf Tower was glittering glass and stood out
in the drab town of Wildpool like a purple-
pink Peruvian parrot in a flock of street starlings.
Inside, the glass corridors were lit with hidden
lamps of pale golds, greens, pinks and purples.
You are wondering how window cleaners could
cope with such a prairie of glass? I can tell you.
Cleaners came in every night and polished and
dusted and cobweb-busted.

Up the fifteen floors they flew on lifts and up
service stairs. These secret stairs were not bright
and glary like the offices and laboratories. They

were painted the colour of sink-trap sludge and lit with weak, beige bulbs.

The stairs opened into half-hidden doors that looked like walls. Except for the fifteenth floor. The door there was locked and a sign said:

KEEP OUT

NO ENTRY FOR UNAUTHORISED PERSONS

DOOR ALARMED

DO NOT TRY TO ENTER

YOU SHOULD NOT EVEN BE READING THIS NOTICE

STOP AT ONCE

RETURN TO THE FOURTEENTH FLOOR OR ELSE

AND DON'T FORGET ... KEEP OUT

The notice was there to keep people out[88].

The rescue team looked over the railings on the roof of Loaf Tower and watched as Arfur

88 You may have guessed that.

Loaf and a woman in red had hurried off towards Dank Alley and Wiggott's Wonderful Waxworld. The team stepped onto the service stairs and crept down. PC Elloe's boots creaked a little – the boots had been new that morning.

They arrived at the door that said *Keep Out*.

'It's alarmed,' Boy said.

'I'm a bit alarmed myself,' the policeman trembled.

'It's just a sign,' Igon the evil assistant Igon told them. 'Arfur Loaf uses this stairway to get to his helicopter on the roof. He can never be bothered to switch the door alarm on.'

Boy nodded. He turned the handle on the door. There was no alarm. He pulled the door towards him. There was no alarm. He opened it wide and felt the warm air of the building wash over him. There was no alarm.

'No alarm,' he said. The others had guessed that.

They stepped into a room of glistening white tiles. In the middle of the room was a glass case – the sort you see in a museum with a long-dead dodo or a shot and snarling stuffed fox glaring out at you through glass eyes.

Marjorie Door and Edna Crudge were there, looking down on her, helpless.

Boy looked at Mrs Crudge and his eyes flew wide open. No one else in the room noticed as she placed a finger quickly to her lips. Boy gave the tiniest of nods and walked towards the centre of the room.

In this case lay a girl. Her face was the face of the girl on the phone. 'Molly Maltby,' Boy said. The others had guessed that too ... in fact Igon KNEW it. But Boy said it anyway. She sprouted wires just as a damp potato sprouts green shoots. She was frowning.

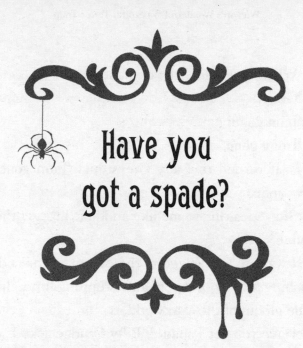

Have you got a spade?

Lady Greystone was wearing red shoes with high heels. *Clack-clack-clack* down the High Street then *clack-clack-eeeek* as they stepped on a rat in dank Alley. Arfur Loaf's black hair bobbed and his white coat flapped. He banged on the back door to Wiggott's with his sledgehammer fist.

Bang-bang-bang-bang. A voice from behind the door said, 'It says knock three times.'

'Just open it, Crudge, or I'll knock your head three times – with a blunt cricket bat,' Loaf said.

The door creaked open. 'No need to turn nasty. I'm only doing my job,' the caretaker said.

'Where is Igon?' Loaf demanded.

'Gone.'

'Igon gone?'

'Long gone.'

Loaf turned to Lady Greystone. 'Igon gone, long gone.'

'Stop speaking to me like an idiot. Just get the phone.'

'I want to see Wiggott,' the evil inventor said, pushing the door open and stepping into the stale gloom of the Waxworld.

'Have you got a spade?' Billy Crudge asked.

'Why do we need a spade to talk to Wiggott?' Lady Greystone asked.

'Because you'll have to dig him up in Wildpool graveyard if you want a word. Mind you, I can't promise he'll talk back.'

'He's dead?' the woman in red asked.

'As Mr Loaf's wig,' Crudge replied.

'When did that happen?'

'About fifty years ago,' the caretaker said. 'Have a look at the gravestone. That'll give you the date.'

'So who runs the Waxworld?' Loaf asked.

'I do. Have done for fifty years.'

Loaf shot out a hand and gripped the brown overall. 'So if you're Wiggott, then you have my phone.'

A sly look crossed Billy Crudge's face. 'The boy-thief stole it from you,' the caretaker said[89].

'And the boy-thief is in your Waxworld,' Loaf said.

'Not any longer he isn't,' Crudge said.

Lady Greystone opened her scarlet handbag and took out a small pistol. She pointed the muzzle between the caretaker's eyes. 'Tell us where he is now, or you will use your brains as Wiggott's Wonderful wallpaper.'

Now Billy Crudge could have saved Boy and Molly and the rescue team. He could have told a big fat lie instead of a sly lie. But looking down the barrel of a gun does strange things to a man's mind. It boggles the brain. Billy Crudge said, 'They flew off to Loaf Tower in a balloon to rescue Molly Maltby.'

Lady Greystone screamed with rage. Arfur Loaf roared. They tumbled over one another to get out of the door and back through Dank Alley to save their prize.

---

89 That was true, of course. Sometimes not telling the whole truth is as sly as telling a lie. A sly lie . . . a 'sl-lie' we could call it.

Lift to
the lift?

Marjorie Door and Edna Crudge stood by the girl in the glass case. 'Well done, Minnie,' they said. 'I knew we could trust you to lead the rescue.'

'We haven't rescued her yet. She's all fastened up in that case. Some of those wires may be keeping her alive. If we unplug her, she may die.'

'Trust me,' Igon said. 'I invented this machine.' He led the way. 'First we pull out the tube from her arm. It has a drug that keeps her body asleep while her brain is awake. It's her brain that powers the phone.'

He raised the glass cover over Molly Maltby. The girl on the table gave a small shudder as the eyepatched man pulled a needle out. 'It will take her ten or fifteen minutes to wake up,' Igon explained. One by one he peeled the plasters that held the wires to her head.

'Arfur Loaf may be back soon,' Edna Crudge said, tense as Robin Hood's bowstring. 'We don't have ten minutes for her to wake and walk to safety.'

'Then we'll have to carry her,' Igon said. 'PC Elloe and you could easily lift her.'

'Where to?' the policeman asked.

'Lift.'

'I know I have to lift her but where to?'

Igon sighed. 'The lift.'

'Lift to the lift?'

'Oh, move out of the way,' Edna Crudge said, taking charge. She lifted Molly gently by the shoulders. 'Marjorie, grab her feet.'

'Are you strong enough?' PC Elloe said, slightly ashamed.

Marjorie looked at him fiercely. 'Young man, I have been knitting for seventy years. Have you any idea how knitting keeps you fit? I have more muscles than Kong King.'

'King Kong?' Elloe said.

'Him as well. Now, Igon, show me to the lift.'

'It's that door in the wall,' the evil assistant said, pointing to a shining metal door that slid open silently as they stepped towards it.

'We'll have to be quick,' Edna said as she lifted the limp Molly off the table and turned towards the lift door.

'You'll have to be quicker than that,' Arfur Loaf chuckled as he stepped from the lift.

'I arrest you for kidnap,' PC Elloe cried.

'I. Don't. Think. So,' Lady Greystone sneered as she pointed her gun at the rescuers.

'You can't get away with it,' the policeman said, pulling handcuffs from his belt. 'You can't shoot us all. . .'

'Yes she can,' Boy snapped.

PC Elloe raised the handcuffs. 'You *can* shoot us all,' he admitted, 'but our brave chief constable, Betterton Nunn, the Bald Eagle, will track you down like . . . like an eagle . . . and bring you to justice.'

That's when Arfur Loaf did something so unexpected the whole room was as speechless as Molly Maltby. He placed his hand on top of his head[90].

---

90 It was so unexpected even I wasn't expecting it. And I thought I knew what was coming next. Just goes to show ... something.

You may as well give up

Even Lady Greystone froze like a grey stone, her mouth with its scarlet lipstick hung open and the gun dropped a little.

Arfur Loaf grasped his thick mane of black bear hair and tugged. It came off like a Yorkshire Terrier in his hand. It was a wig ... but you'd guessed that ... and his bald head glinted under the pale lights. A head as bald as a billiard ball, as bald as an egg, as bald as a head with no hair.

His evil eyes glinted twice as bright. 'So, Constable Lawrence Olivier Elloe, can you see why I am not afraid of Chief Constable Betterton Nunn?'

'Yes, sir,' Elloe breathed. 'Under that black wig you are...'

'I am...

Say it.'

'You are...'

'Yes?'

'You are B-B-B-Betterton Nunn.'

'Hah! It's true,' the evil man cried and flung the wig to the floor, where it didn't whine or yap like a black Yorkshire Terrier. 'I control the police. When Igon came to me with a plan to make millions – a plan that meant kidnapping a kid – then I knew there would be a fuss. I knew you couldn't swipe a boy or girl off the street without a huge search. But that was the clever part of my plan.'

Boy nodded. 'You sent your police looking in all the wrong places.'

Nunn grinned. 'Not only that, but I told them NOT to look in Loaf Tower. I said Arfur Loaf was the kindest citizen in the whole of Wildpool.'

'But you didn't reckon on Boy stealing the infinit-G phone,' Igon said.

Arfur Loaf breathed heavily and angrily. 'I didn't. And to make it worse there were no police left to look for it . . . only some new, young idiot on his first day.'

PC Elloe jangled his handcuffs. Lady Greystone raised her pistol so it pointed at him. 'But your new, young idiot on his first day not only found the phone,' PC Elloe said proudly, 'he found the girl too.'

'And the Ladies Who Crunch have saved her,' Edna Crudge said just as proudly.

Minnie said, 'You're finished, Betterton Nunn. We have the girl, Wiggott has the phone. You may as well give up.'

'Ha, no! I still have Igon's plans. I can just escape with Lady Stray-broke's millions and set up in a new town with a new kidnap.'

PC Elloe shook his head. 'You can't get away,' he said.

Betterton Nunn snorted. 'Easy. I'll just send for the police helicopter. They still think I'm the chief constable. They'll land on the helipad above us and fly us off to Greystone Castle.'

Minnie Cooper threw back her old head

and laughed. 'They can't land on the roof. Our balloon is up there.'

Lady Greystone backed towards the lift, still waving the pistol. 'Then we'll take the balloon. Grab a Lady Who Crunches, Betterton,' she said.

The chief constable took hold of Marjorie Door's arm and pulled her over to the lift. Her knitting needles rattled like runaway false teeth. 'If you call the police in the next hour, then the old lady gets a bullet in the brain.'

'You'll have trouble finding a brain in there,' Edna sniffed. But the villain and his scarlet lady were gone with the Crunching Lady and the lift doors closed.

'We've saved the girl but lost the criminal,' PC Elloe groaned. 'To think I never saw the biggest clue of all.'

Boy nodded. 'Yes, it's true after all. Arfur Loaf IS Betterton Nunn[91].'

---

91 Yes, YOU saw that clue right from the start. Clever you.

Throw her out
of the basket?

Betterton Nunn pressed the lift button to
take him to the roof. His head was shining
with sweat. Lady Greystone just looked annoyed.
'This did not go to plan, Mr Nunn.'

'Only because that idiot policeman got lucky.
And we were *un*-lucky to be robbed by that boy.
Next time we kidnap someone who won't be
missed.'

The woman in red nodded. 'That's what the
bodysnatchers Burke and Hare did[92].'

'And we tell nobody about our plan. Someone
in Loaf Tower spilled the beans about the

---

92 This wicked woman had studied the history of crime. Who says
learning history is useless?

infinit-G phone and Wiggott got to hear about it.'

The lift hissed to a halt and the door opened.

They stepped out onto the roof, where the balloon smoked in the hazy evening sun. The sky was as clear as it ever got over Wildpool.

'This old woman knows about our plans,' Lady Greystone said, poking her gun at Marjorie Door. 'What do you plan to do with her? Lift off through the clouds then throw her out of the basket?'

Nunn gave a savage grin. 'I have just had an even better idea. When we get to Greystone Castle we set up a new laboratory. We build a new phone then we find a new living brain to power it.'

Lady Greystone's eyes went as hard as rubies. 'And this time we won't need to kidnap some girl and make a fuss.' The rubies turned towards Marjorie Door. 'This time we use the brain of a Lady Who Crunches.'

Marjorie raised her eyebrows. 'Oh, how kind. It is an honour to know my brains are so powerful. Edna can be very cruel, you know. She says I'm only fit to knit. I'm a knit-wit, she says.'

But Nunn wasn't listening. He took a fire-axe from beside the door and started to smash the door to the stairs into firewood. He threw it onto the smoking embers in the balloon's fire-basket and used bellows to puff it into a mass of hot air.

The ropes creaked and stretched. Lady Greystone lifted Marjorie into the basket. The Crunching Lady wafted a hand in front of her wrinkled, crinkled old face. 'I always feel a little giddy when I fly. Excuse me if I tie my scarf to this thick rope and wrap it around me. My scarf is my anchor. It will make me feel safe and sick-free.'

'Do what you like,' the scarlet-dressed woman snapped.

Marjorie did what she liked and smiled peacefully. 'Mind you,' Marjorie said as Nunn untied the rope that held the balloon down to the helipad. 'It's a lovely evening for a balloon flight isn't it?'

Her captor swung her head round and said, 'Stop talking or I will stuff a ball of wool into your mouth. Understand?'

Marjorie said nothing.

'Understand? Answer me,' the stone-hearted Greystone shouted. 'Why don't you answer?'

'Because you told me not to say anything,' Marjorie said gently.

The lady's red lips were tight as a stab mark. The balloon lifted off the roof and the sunset breeze drifted it towards the north-east and Greystone Castle. Marjorie Door said nothing. But inside she was laughing very, very loudly.

It was all a nightmare

'What can we do to rescue Marjorie?' Edna Crudge sighed. 'If we run downstairs and call the police that Cray-cone woman will shoot her.'

'Marjorie is not the knit-wit you keep saying she is,' Minnie Cooper said. 'Marjorie is sharp as a knitting needle. She'll find a way out.'

Boy shook his head. 'I'm an expert on escapes, but even I can't think of a way out of a balloon fifty metres in the air with a gun pointed at my head.'

Minnie grinned. 'You're not Marjorie. Wait and see.'

'Then we need to call the police,' Igon said.

'I *am* the police,' PC Elloe said. He was a little huffed and hurt.

'I mean the *real* police. The ones who can send up the police helicopter to capture the balloon,' Igon said.

The policeman turned pink[93]. 'I should arrest you for being part of Arfur Loaf's evil plans,' he said.

'And I could report you for flying a balloon without a pilot's licence,' Igon spat back.

'Stop squabbling and squibbling and squirmishing and let's squidaddle out of this place,' Edna Crudge said.

'We can't just leave Molly,' Boy argued.

'You and the pathetic policeman can carry her,' Mrs Crudge said.

'She'll wake soon, I reckon,' Igon said.

'But where are we going?' Minnie Cooper cried.

'To Greystone Castle to rescue Miss Door,' PC Elloe said.

The policeman and the thief lifted Molly, who started to moan as her milk-pale face began to turn a healthy shade of blancmange pink.

---

93 Only his face. Not his navy blue uniform with silver buttons.

The rescuers hurried into the lift as Molly began to wriggle. By the time they had reached the ground floor she was blinking in the sunset light that was flooding through the glass walls of the great tower. She looked at Boy. 'I think I know you,' she murmured. 'I had the strangest dream of pirates and bodysnatchers, monks and balloons.'

'It was all a nightmare,' Minnie Cooper said gently, 'but you're safe now. We'll explain later. But for now we have to rescue an old friend of mine.'

'Rescue from where?' Molly asked.

'From Greystone Castle,' PC Elloe said.

'Where's that?' Molly asked.

There was silence. Then Igon, Edna Crudge, PC Elloe and Boy answered, together, '*I* don't know.'

It didn't matter much, because Marjorie Door wasn't headed for the mysteriously missing Greystone Castle...

Coo-ee

The setting sun shone red on the head of Betterton Nunn and turned Lady Greystone's dress even redder. The evil inventor's eyes looked dreamy. 'It was good being a millionaire,' he sighed, 'but it will be even better to be a billionaire.'

'So long as those nuisance people in Loaf Tower don't call the police before we land. We aren't moving very fast,' the lady complained.

'They won't dare follow. Not while we have a hostage,' Nunn cooed like a dove. Below them Wildpool looked like a toy village and even the grubby streets were as cute as dolls' houses. 'Of course, we'll need to make sure they don't trace us to your castle.'

'They will never find Greystone Castle,' the lady in red replied. 'It's not on any map and it's mostly underground. From above it looks like an ancient ruin.'

'An ancient ruin? A bit like the Lady Who Crunches ... the one we kidnapped,' Nunn chuckled. 'Isn't that right, Miss Door?' he laughed cruelly and turned to look at Marjorie.

Marjorie didn't reply. Marjorie couldn't reply. Marjorie wasn't there.

'She's gone,' Nunn wailed. 'Our hostage is gone. She can't have jumped overboard. She didn't have a parachute. She'll be crushed on the cobbles below ... or crashed through some tiles. She really will be a lady who crunched[94].'

Lady Greystone took two steps across the basket and looked at where Marjorie had been standing. 'She used her never-ending scarf to slide down and escape. Look, she tied it to the side of the basket.'

---

94 That's not a bad joke for a man as deathly serious as Betterton Nunn. A rather unkind joke, mind. Especially if you were walking down the street and Marjorie crunched on top of you.

Nasty Nunn joined her and looked down. Marjorie was standing on the top of Wildpool Church tower. 'Coo-ee,' she called and waved up at them.

'She's tied the scarf to the church flagpole,' Greystone groaned. 'No wonder we aren't moving very fast.'

'If the rescuers see her they'll send for the police to haul us down, lock us up and ruin my billionaire plans,' the chief constable complained.

'We need to unfasten the scarf from that church tower,' Lady Greystone said, urgent and close to panic.

'You'll have to climb down and unfasten it,' Nunn said, and his powerful voice was even more of a panicking squeak.

'I can't climb down the scarf,' his partner in crime said. 'I'm wearing a dress. The people on the ground will see my knickers. *You'll* have to do it.'

Nunn nodded. 'It's the only way,' he agreed. He lifted a leg over the side of the basket and began to slide down the scarf like a zip-wire in a play-park. When he was halfway down he called back up, 'No, your ladyship. There is another way. We could just unfasten the scarf from the basket.'

The woman nodded, said, 'Good idea,' and began to unfasten the knot.

'Not now!' Nunn screamed. 'I'll fall and smash into the graveyard.'

'Ohhhh ... then climb back up,' she raged. 'Idiot. You should have thought of that before you set off.' But climbing back up was harder than climbing down.

Marjorie waved and cried 'Coo-ee!' from the church tower again while the rescuers gathered in the streets of Wildpool below.

'Well done, knit-wit,' Edna called up to the top of the church tower. 'We've trapped them.'

'Not for long,' Boy muttered. 'Not for long.'

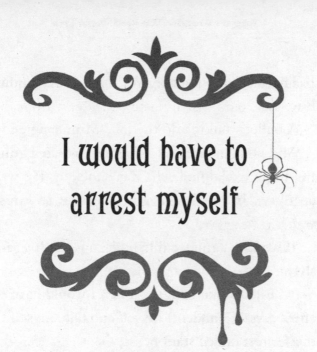

I would have to
arrest myself

'The Boy's right,' Edna Crudge said. 'Arfur Loaf will climb back up the scarf – I'm not sure why he slid down – they'll untie it then float off into the sky.'

'We'll follow them,' Boy said.

'It'll be too dark soon,' Minnie Cooper pointed out. 'Even the police helicopter couldn't find them. It'll be morning before they find the balloon and those roguish, rapscalliony, crooked kidnappers will be long gone.'

'There's only one thing for it,' Edna said. 'We'll have to shoot it down. Punch a hole in the balloon and let the hot air escape.'

The rescuers gasped. 'We don't have a gun,' Boy said.

'A bullet wouldn't do the job,' Minnie agreed.

'And no one here has a licence to own a gun,' PC Elloe exclaimed. He was shocked. He was on duty. 'If you had a gun I'd have to arrest you.'

'If we had a gun we'd hand it to you,' Boy said slyly.

PC Elloe looked angry. 'Then I would have to arrest myself, handcuff myself and take myself to the nearest police station.'

Molly was wobbly on her feet still and her voice was vague. 'A cannon would do the job,' she said.

The others looked at her. 'It would,' Minnie nodded. 'Do you need a licence to fire a cannon, officer?' she asked the policeman.

'I … erm… I … erm… I'm not sure that problem has ever come up in Wildpool,' he admitted.

'You'll never get to be chief constable if you don't know the law,' Boy jeered. PC Elloe glowered.

'We don't have a cannon, so it doesn't matter,' Edna snapped.

'But,' Molly said and rubbed her forehead. 'In my dream – my weird dream – I was on a pirate ship. And PC Elloe here fired a cannon.'

'That was in Wiggott's Wonderful Waxworld,' Elloe answered.

'Then it'll still be there,' Boy said. 'Let's get it.'

Before anyone could argue they seemed to have agreed. Boy and the policeman would run to Dank Alley and collect the cannon while the other three waited under the church tower.

Betterton Nunn was still struggling up the scarf as Boy sprinted through the town and PC Elloe clopped along in his big boots after him. It was a race against time – it was a race against Nunn, it was a race against the darkness and a race against the rose-red, setting sun. Who would win[95]?

95 Don't ask me. I haven't read the end of the story.

We haven't time

In the caverns and the canyons of the old city there were places where the sun was almost afraid to shine. Dank Alley was such a place. But for five minutes, at the end of a clear day, the low setting sun managed to creep down the cobbles for a few final moments before darkness closed its cloak and the rats ran riot.

Boy and PC Elloe slithered between the tall walls of the alley that were of warped wood and soot-stained stone. They splashed through puddles.

The sign read *Wiggott's Wonderful Waxworld.*

Underneath, even fainter writing said *Deliveries – Knock three times.*

Knock-knock. Nothing. No one answered. PC Elloe rapped with his truncheon. Nothing. Time was ticking by.

Boy pushed at the door. It wasn't locked. He ran into the green gloom of the Waxworld. Billy Crudge the caretaker was in his little office, his head bent over the infinit-G phone. He had a tiny screwdriver in his hand and an eyeglass in his eye like a jeweller.

'We need to borrow the cannon from the naval ship in the Blackbeard scene,' Elloe said, breathless.

'But we don't want to get caught up in a sea battle. We haven't time,' Boy added.

The caretaker waved a hand. 'Then don't take the train and enter through the front of the Waxworld. Take the service passage through that door over there. It leads to the back doors of the Waxworlds. The animatronics don't come alive if you go in that way.'

Boy ran through the door and ran down a dim corridor with a greasy light bulb giving the only light and spiders watching from the cream glass lampshade. They entered a room with twenty sides and twenty doors. Each door had a label: *Burke and Hare's Edinburgh*, *Charles Dickens's London* and so on. At last Boy found *Blackbeard's cabin* and *Captain Maynard's cabin*.

Boy rushed through the last of these and past the Waxworld dummies till he was on the deck of the naval ship. The cannon on the deck was a small one on wheels. He pulled it easily towards the door calling, 'Get a couple of cannonballs, a bag of gunpowder and a length of fuse, constable.'

Elloe obeyed. They ran back through the twenty-sided room and down the corridor, past Billy Crudge's office.

'We'll bring it back,' the lawful Elloe said.

The caretaker waved a careless hand and shrugged, then got on with his task of taking the phone apart.

The light was almost gone from Dank Alley as the two gunners sped along. Rats shivered in the shadows[96].

Boy and Elloe raced to the church, where four

---

96 Those intrepid rodents laughed at cats and rat-traps set to catch them ... but a cannon was serious. They didn't know it wasn't meant for them.

worried watchers looked up at the balloon above them. Stars were appearing in the purple sky but the rescue team could make out a bald-headed man in the basket, grinning down at them.

He was untying the scarf that held it to the church tower's flagpole. He pulled it free of the balloon basket and let the top of the scarf drop. That was a big mistake. No – it was a B-I-G mistake.

Sadly, the cannon doesn't have wings

The balloon was beginning to rise. It was drifting away on a night breeze as the moon began to rise too.

Boy set the cannon on a gravestone. A stone angel stared at him. He rested the muzzle of the cannon on the angel's shoulder and packed in powder from Elloe's pouch, then a cannonball. He placed a fuse in the firing hole and struck one of Blackbeard's beard matches. He looked along the barrel to make sure the balloon was in its sights, then placed his fingers in his ears.

They all did. There was a mighty flash and

a bang loud enough to wake people sleeping underground.

The rays of the rising moon glowed silver on the cannonball as it rose into the air. As it rose, Nunn froze. The silver shape hung there like a bonfire rocket and then, just before it reached the basket, it began to fall, slowly at first. Then with a whistle it dropped out of sight. There was a moment of silence then a shattering clashing of breaking glass. There was a short hush. Nearly as short as Igon.

'We missed,' Igon said.

'Not by much,' Boy moaned. 'If we were just twenty metres higher we'd have hit him.'

'The church tower's twenty metres higher,' Molly said.

She sounded like the know-all girl on the phone and Boy bristled as he had in the Waxworlds. 'Sadly, the cannon doesn't have wings to fly to the top of the tower,' he snarled.

'There are stairs,' Igon said eagerly. He ran across to the church door, turned the handle and pushed with his shoulder. 'Ouch,' he cried. In the battle between an evil assistant's shoulder and an old oak door, the door won. 'It's locked,' he groaned.

'The scarf,' Molly said. 'He left the scarf behind. Use it to pull the cannon up to the roof[97].'

The gun crew called to Marjorie and she lowered the scarf while Boy tied it to the smoking cannon. Marjorie heaved, she panted and she gasped. 'I'm strong, but I'm not that strong,' she shouted down.

Igon ran to the foot of the wall, grasped the scarf and scaled it like a monkey. Boy and Molly followed. They felt the breeze on their cheeks. It was shifting direction and blowing the balloon back towards the centre of Wildpool. As they struggled to the top of the tower they saw the balloon loom larger over them till it blotted out the moon.

'We're bound to hit it now,' Igon gloated. 'A couple of shots should do it.'

'We only have one,' PC Elloe said. 'I could only carry two cannonballs from the Waxworld.'

'One shot, Boy,' Molly said. 'Do you think you can do it?'

Boy loaded the cannon carefully and rested it

97 See? I told you Nunn shouldn't have let the scarf drop. Untying it was not a good idea . . . or knot a good idea.

on the wall till it was pointing above the basket. He raised the match. His hand was trembling.

'Spare us, please, spare us,' Betterton Nunn wailed. Boy lowered the match towards the fuse.

We, the hunted, will now hunt

Boy looked at Molly. 'I may hit Nunn or Greystone by mistake,' he said.

She gripped his arm. 'What would William Burke have done? What would Blackbeard have said?'

Boy nodded slowly. 'Belay those hornpipes, stow yer deadlights, hornswaggle the hempen halter, grab your grapeshot, scrape the barnacles off me rudder and shiver me timbers, me hearties, me picaroons, me scallywag rapscalliony buckos. And remember . . . fried eggs tell no lies.'

'Would he worry about hitting a villain like Nunn?'

'I'm not Blackbeard,' Boy said quietly. 'I'm not William Burke. I'm a thief, not a killer.'

Then there was a singing, zinging, whistling pinging as Lady Greystone fired her pistol and the bullet bounced off the top of the church tower.

'No, but that woman is Helen Burke. The next bullet may kill one of us.'

The next bullet made a *thlurrrrp* as it landed in the lead on the roof.

Molly took boy's hand and together they moved the match towards the fuse. 'Remember Captain Blood, then. He was a thief, not a killer. What did *he* say?'

'We, the hunted, will now hunt,' Boy muttered.

The two hands pressed the match against the fuse. It sizzled and hissed, hizzled and sissed, then went silent as the flame disappeared into the hole in the cannon.

The gunpowder exploded, the cannon kicked and the roof shook. Betterton Nunn ducked and even Lady Greystone lowered her pistol to watch the flight of the cannonball. It roared, then it soared. There was a spitting, splitting sound as it tore through the balloon at one side and then exploded out of the other side.

Seconds later there was a distant shattering clashing of breaking glass. 'Somebody's greenhouse lost a window or twenty,' Minnie sighed as she looked up from the graveyard[98].

Slowly, slowly, the balloon seemed to shrink and dropped towards the field next to the church. It stopped casting its moon-shadow and the watchers on the top of the tower were dazzled by the silver disc in the sky.

The great blue balloon settled in the field. The fire-basket scattered its embers upwards as the silk and paper balloon fell onto it and was set alight. The fire that the burning balloon made was brighter than the moon.

The watchers were dazzled. Too dazzled to see two shadows limp and hobble away from the crash and vanish into the dark hedgerows and the lanes that led towards the hills.

By the time the Wildpool Fire Service had clanged and rattled and sloshed its way to the scene there was hardly anyone for PC Elloe to arrest.

---

98 Yes, twenty greenhouse windows shattered. Very sad. Those cannon-firing fools should have been more careful. It wasn't just the windows. Hundreds of greenhouse tomatoes died that night in the chill, dark air. A tomatoey tragedy.

Igon had melted as mysteriously as his master into the ink of the night, his black clothes a perfect camouflage. That left Boy.

The thief spread his hands. 'You could arrest me for stealing a phone, but where is it now? And where is the man who said I'd pinched it?'

The police sergeant with the big moustache had arrived with Molly's parents. They smothered their lost daughter with hugs and soaked her hair with tears. They dragged her off home before she could stop them. 'There's someone I need to say goodbye to,' she argued.

'That can wait,' Mrs Maltby sniffed and pulled Molly down the path to home.

The police sergeant wrapped an arm around PC Elloe's narrow shoulders. 'You are a wonder of Wildpool Police,' he said. 'You found the girl when all the force around you failed.'

'But the villains got away,' Elloe sighed. 'And I think somebody's pinched my bike.'

'Never mind that. Come back to the station. The mayor and half of Wildpool wants to say hello, L.O. Elloe.'

'But the thief...' Elloe began. But Boy

was gone – as gone as Igon – into the moon-shadows.

The Ladies Who Crunch wandered back through the town of Wildpool. In the gossiping streets the excited people were still talking about the great blue balloon that had soared over their heads and then crashed in flames. It was more fun than the day of the boat race on Wildpool canal when the crews crashed and sank. Oh, how they had laughed that day.

'It was a Montgolfier balloon, I tell you,' one man was telling his son as they walked past the three old ladies.

'But where did it come from, Dad?' the boy whinged and whined.

'Probably the toyshop on Canal Road.'

'But it was huge, Dad. It wasn't a toy. There were people in it and they were firing guns.'

'They were firing blanks,' the man said. 'It was all part of a movie. Yes, that's what it was.'

'How do you know, Dad?'

'Because I'm a teacher, son. I know everything.'

And they went off home to tea. They would

look up 'Montgolfier balloons' on the internet and the dad would make the boy write an essay about them.

Marjorie Door stopped at the corner of the High Street. 'I need to buy some more wool before the shops close for the night,' she told her crunching friends.

'That scarf of yours did a wonderful job,' Minnie said.

Marjorie sighed. 'It's ruined now – stretched with all that climbing up and down. I'll buy some new knitting needles and start again tomorrow.'

'Another scarf?' Edna Crudge asked.

'No, a new cardigan for Minnie here. She earned a treat after chasing those villains through the creepy Waxworlds.'

Minnie smiled. 'Thank you, Marjorie. You were very brave yourself. Right, I'll get off home. There's a programme on the telly I want to watch about cars.'

'Cars? What sort of cars?' Edna asked.

'Mini Coopers, of course,' her friend replied.

'It's been an exciting day,' Minnie said to herself as she shuffled along to her little house.

'*It has*,' she answered. 'You're talking to yourself again. *I know. But when you're old and lonely it's nice to hear a friendly voice.* Even if it's your own? *Even if it's your own. Time for cocoa.*' She toddled off tired (but happy) to the empty house where she hid from the doctors who ran the old people's home.

Edna still had work to do. She pushed her shoulders back and marched off towards the dark side of Wildpool, where even the police were afraid to patrol. Unless the policeman was PC Elloe, of course. It's not that he was so very brave. He was simply stupid and didn't know who might be hiding behind that green lamp post[99].

She looked over her shoulder to see if she was being followed. She wasn't. She slipped into the darkest street of all.

99 Who hides behind a green lamp post? A very skinny child playing hide and seek ... or a skinny wolf waiting for Red Riding Hood. Luckily, there weren't any wolves in Wildpool.

What's in
a name?

The Master-Thief's house stood on a shabby Wildpool street. The street lamp outside was broken-dark and the pavement cracked. When someone stumbled in the dark the cracked stone clacked and warned the Master-Thief inside that a stranger was prowling there.

Boy knew the street like an old postman knows the gardens with the wildest Wildpool dogs. He stepped carefully over the pavement till he reached the front door.

He slipped a key into the well-oiled lock. It

opened silently, yet still the Master-Thief knew he was there.

Boy's teacher and guardian sat in a room lit with only a single candle. 'Come in, Boy.'

'I delivered the phone to Wiggott's,' he said.

'I know. You did well. It wasn't easy. One day you'll be a Master-Thief and sit at this very table, counting your well-earned gains. Do you have the money?'

Boy placed the packet of one thousand pounds on the table. The Master-Thief counted out five hundred and pushed it across the table to Boy. Boy did not say thanks. That's one thing they don't teach you at thief school. You can see why. You can't really pick a pocket or two and say, 'Thank you for being so careless with your purse and making me so happy.'

'There's supper on the kitchen table. It's a shepherd's pie.'

'Did you pinch it from a shepherd?' Boy said and a crooked smile crossed his face. It was an old joke he'd shared with the Master-Thief for years.

'No, I shot the shepherd and minced him up,'

the Master-Thief cackled. Another old joke. 'Your bed's ready upstairs,' the Master-Thief went on. 'You must be exhausted. I put in a hot-water bottle for you. Can I get anything else for you before I go to my own dinner?'

Boy nodded slowly. 'I'd like to read a book by Charles Dickens. He seems to be an ... interesting writer. He didn't write about great and good people. He wrote about people from the dark streets with darker secrets. People like me.'

The Master-Thief nodded and tapped the screen of a small pad on the desk. 'There you go. I've downloaded *Oliver Twist* for you.'

Boy grinned. 'Perfect, thanks.'

He took the reader and headed for the kitchen, where the shepherd's pie was waiting for him. The Master-Thief rose stiffly from the table. 'I'd better get home – it's my turn to cook dinner tonight. Mr Crudge will be late. He has a lot of work to do on that phone before he finishes for the day.'

'So, is your husband Billy Crudge ... or is he Dr Wiggott?' Boy asked.

Edna shrugged. 'Why can't he be both? The same as Arfur Loaf can be Betterton Nunn ... and I can be your Master-Thief or Edna Crudge. What's in a name, as a famous writer once said.'

'Charles Dickens?'

'No. William Shakespeare. You can read him another day. Goodnight, Boy.'

'Goodnight, Mrs Crudge,' Boy said and went wearily off to his supper and bed.

Pfffffffffffffffththththtttt.

Lady Greystone's red high-heeled shoe stuck in a boggy part of the field and came off. She threw away the other one and squelched on in her silk stockings, which were as ruined as the silk on the burning balloon. 'Not far now, Betterton,' she said.

The large man struggled on, driven by rage like a Montgolfier balloon was driven by smoke. 'Next time, Lady Grey-smoke, we'll come up with a plan that will make us richer than Croesus.'

'Creosote? Who's he?'

'Who-oooo,' an owl hooted.

'A Greek king. The richest man in the world at that time.'

'I like that,' Lady Greystone hissed. If she had listened to her teacher she'd have known that Croesus came to a very nasty end. His son died horribly, too. Lady Greystone should have learned: money can't buy you happiness ... but it can buy you jelly babies, which is pretty much the same thing. 'So what's your new plan?'

'I saw a movie where there was a clever fat man with a bald head...'

'That'll be you,' the lady in the muddy red dress said.

'...He robbed the biggest gold store in the world,' Nunn said.

'And did he get away with it?'

'N-n-noooo. But only because a spy called James Bond stopped him. His name was Goldfinger.'

'I though you said his name was James Bond,' her ladyship said.

'No, the gold thief was called Goldfinger.'

'You can't buy much if you just have a finger made of gold,' she sniffed.

'Noooo ... that was his nickname because he

loved gold. Bond killed him in the end,' Nunn explained.

Lady Greystone nodded. 'So how do we stop this James Bond killing us?' she asked.

'Aha, that's where my plan is so clever. James Bond can't kill us because he's just a character in a book.'

The lady nodded. 'And what are we?'

'We're real people,' Nunn said and tugged his partner-in-crime out of a deep sinkhole of mud. 'It'll work, you'll see,' the large man said.

In the moonlight the ruin of an old castle loomed. 'We're there,' the woman sighed. 'Greystone Castle. Time for a hot cup of tea and then our new plan to get rich.'

'Who-oooo.'

'Us, of course. You have the brains,' she said.

'And you have Nunn,' he replied.

He was worth a thousand times more

In Dank Alley the cobbles had come to life.
Rats raced round with prizes stolen from the gutters outside the fish shop. Cats raced round after the rats and dogs chased after the cats. Only an ancient gas lamp glowed greenish-white above the sign on the warped wooden door. Once it had been rich red with golden letters. Once it had read *Wiggott's Wonderful Waxworld*. Underneath, even fainter writing said *Deliveries – Knock three times*. No one knocked.

But if you were to push that door open you'd find it quiet inside. There was the quiet sound of dust settling on the animatronic figures in the Waxworlds and the trains. Nothing stirred in the stillness now. Except...

In a little office Billy Crudge the caretaker used a pair of tweezers to lift up a tiny copper chip from inside a phone that lay on his desk. 'This is it,' he said. 'This is the computer chip that makes computers act like real human beings. Forget infinit-G phones. Put chips like these into Wiggott's animatronics and they will be a sensation. People will come from every corner of the Earth to see Wiggott's Wonderful Waxworld again.'

He dropped the wonderful chip into an envelope and rose to his feet, stiff with sitting too long. He rubbed his eyes, tired with squinting too hard. 'Better get back to our Edna,' he said. 'She says it's shepherd's pie for dinner tonight. And I'll bet she says she pinched it from a shepherd.' He chuckled. 'She always says that.'

He walked towards the door that led to the room at the back of the Waxworlds. He didn't need to read the labels. He knew which door he wanted. The label read *The Waxworld of Ikey*

Solomon[100]. He tapped on the door. 'Enter,' came the voice.

Billy opened the door, stepped in and smiled. 'I have it here,' he said, waving the envelope with the computer chip inside.

'Well done, Billy,' the shady figure behind a great green-covered desk said. 'It's been a good day.'

'A good day, though I didn't think the animatronics would give us so much trouble.'

'You paid the boy-thief his thousand pounds,' the figure said.

'I did. He was worth every penny.'

'He was worth a thousand times more ... but don't tell the Master-Thief that.'

Billy Crudge threw back his head and laughed at a joke only he and the figure understood. 'No. Oh, no. More than my life's worth ... speaking of the Master-Thief, I'd better get back home. Dinner will be on the table soon, I expect.'

'Shepherd's pie. You've earned your dinner. We start a new life tomorrow, Billy... Tomorrow is the first day of the all-new, all-amazing,

---

100 I know what you're going to say ... I told you that he didn't read the labels. I am saying the label WOULD have said that if he HAD read it. Got that? Good.

Wiggott's Wonderful Waxworld. Time to go now, though. I'll lock up on my way out ... we don't want any thieves in here.'

Billy Crudge laughed. 'We don't. I'll see you later, then.'

'See you later, Billy.'

'See you later, Dr Wiggott.'

More from Terry Deary

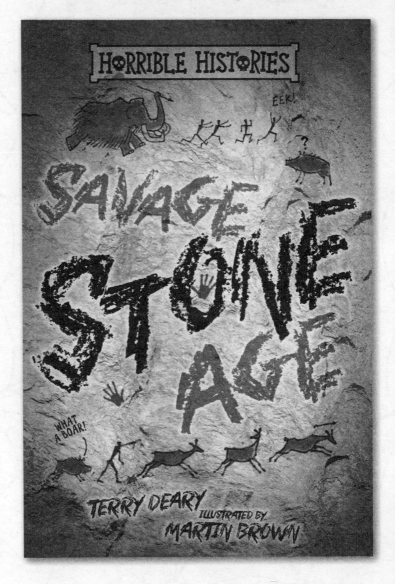

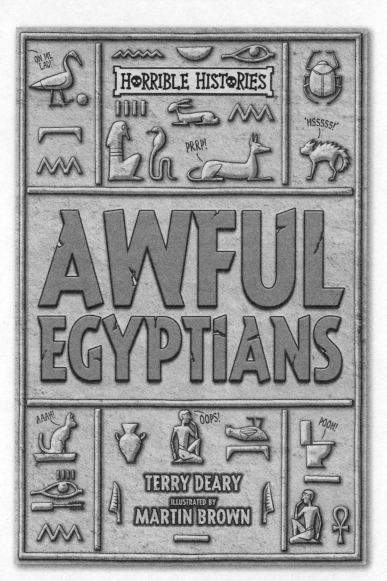

HORRIBLE HISTORIES

AWFUL EGYPTIANS

TERRY DEARY

ILLUSTRATED BY
MARTIN BROWN

HORRIBLE HISTORIES

GROOVY GREEKS

I THOUGHT IT WOULD BE BIGGER

TERRY DEARY

ILLUSTRATED BY MARTIN BROWN

ROTTEN ROMANS

MURMILLOS
ARE THE BEST

CAESAR WAS
'ERE

ROMAN LIONS
RULE!

TERRY DEARY ILLUSTRATED BY MARTIN BROWN

HORRIBLE HISTORIES

VICIOUS VIKINGS

EEK

ARE WE NEARLY THERE YET?

TERRY DEARY

Illustrated by Martin Brown

HORRIBLE HISTORIES
MEOW
Measly Middle Ages
OUCH
Terry Deary
Illustrated by Martin Brown

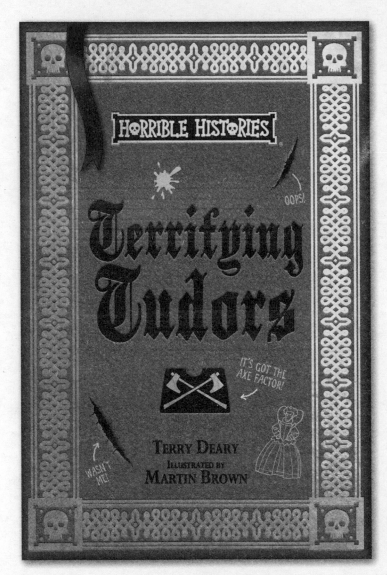

HORRIBLE HISTORIES

OOPS!

Terrifying
Tudors

IT'S GOT THE
AXE FACTOR!

WASN'T
ME!

TERRY DEARY

ILLUSTRATED BY
MARTIN BROWN

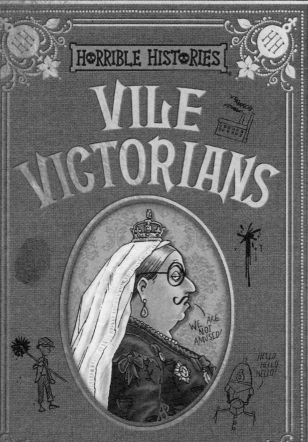

HORRIBLE HISTORIES

VILE VICTORIANS

WE ARE NOT AMUSED!

HELLO HELLO HELLO!

TERRY DEARY

ILLUSTRATED BY **MARTIN BROWN**

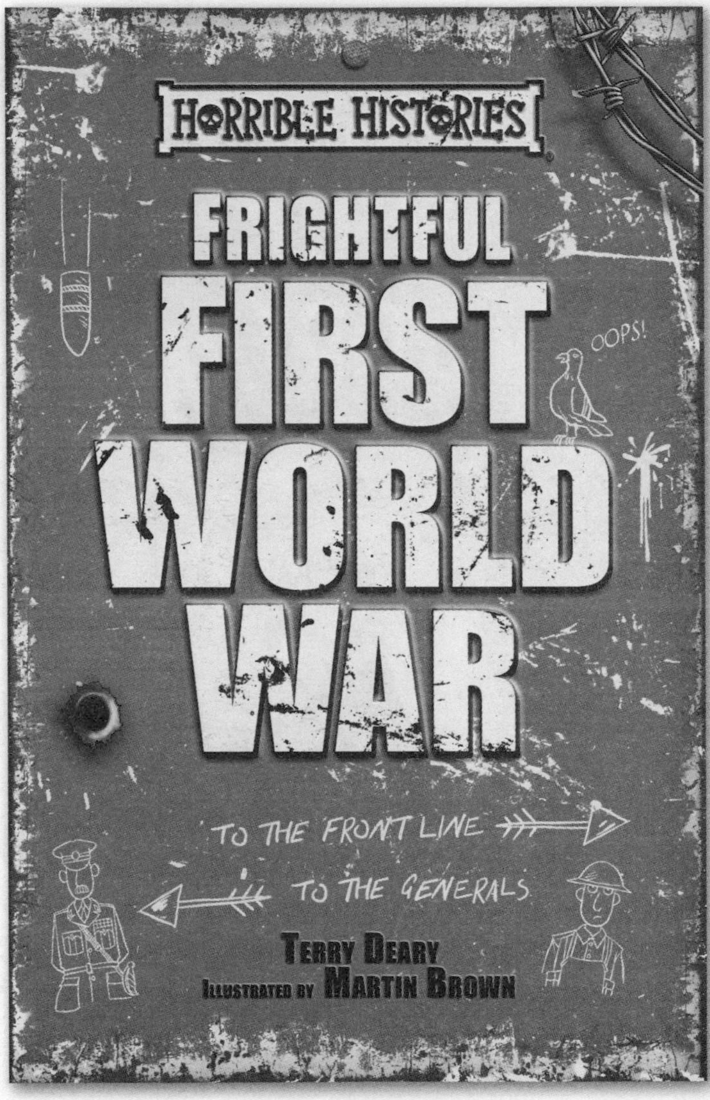

HORRIBLE HISTORIES

FRIGHTFUL
FIRST
WORLD
WAR

OOPS!

TO THE FRONT LINE >>>

<<< TO THE GENERALS

TERRY DEARY

ILLUSTRATED BY **MARTIN BROWN**

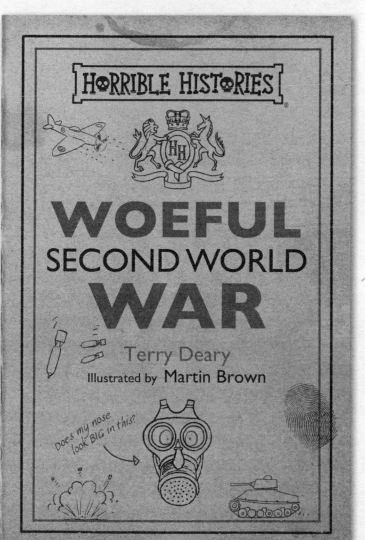

HORRIBLE HISTORIES

WOEFUL
SECOND WORLD
WAR

Terry Deary

Illustrated by **Martin Brown**

Does my nose look BIG in this?